ETERNAL

JUSTICE

Author:
R. L. Dodson

Dedicated to
My Father

Eternal Justice

R. L. Dodson

Copyright 2014 by R L Dodson

All rights reserved.

ISBN-13: 978-1495326561
ISBN-10: 149532656X

This book is a work of fiction. Names, characters, places and incidents are either the product of the author's imagination or are used fictitiously. Any resemblances to actual events, locales, or persons, living or dead are entirely coincidental.

Prologue

St. Andrews Bay, Florida
8:30 p.m.

Hurricane warnings spread across the whole Florida Coast. Jagged streaks of lightning painted the night sky as the rain came pelting down. The wind had picked up significantly, gusting at sixty five miles per hour, as the team made their way to their assigned locations. Operation Sundown was underway. Too much manpower and too much money had been expended to call the operation at this late date. Joint agency efforts, including Drug Enforcement Administration, Federal Bureau of Investigation, Navy Seals, and CIA, were all present in great numbers tonight.

The CIA undercover operative had successfully infiltrated the Martinelli Drug Cartel. It had taken years to get in this deep. Ashley looked through her night-vision goggles once more, silently scanning the terrain below. Anthony, the operative, had entered the room with Martinelli and an old silver-haired man. This was the largest shipment the Colombian Cartel had brought into the United States. Drug Cartel henchmen were positioned in front and strategically located throughout the warehouse. Several were also waiting for the ships at the docks behind the warehouse.

"Anthony is in over his head. I don't believe his alias of Victor Shayne is as solid as he believes." Ashley said.

Something that resembled concern tugged at Chase's gut. He managed to paste on a mask of assurance and responded to his partner.

"Anthony is the best undercover agent I know; he worked with the DEA for years before defecting over to the CIA. He will do fine. He hasn't spent all these years undercover not to know his enemy. You both can work out your differences later."

Ashley examined her partner and best friend's face and saw the worry flickering in his steel gray eyes. Her panic deepened. "I'm still in love with him and I never told him he has a son. I have so many regrets. But, all of that put aside, this operation just doesn't feel right." Her features grew pained, as if the admission caused her physical torture.

Chase silenced her with a sympathetic look. "Stop," he ordered. "It's pointless flinging the past at each other. You and Anthony just need to clear the air." His voice suddenly sounded strained. "Seriously, Ashley, what do you want?"

"I want this operation to be over. And I want Anthony to be safe."

He frowned, looking at the monitors in the van all blinking and recording every movement of Anthony in the warehouse below. "We'll figure it out." His voice reassured her that everything would be okay.

Ashley continued to study the monitors and adjusted the volume to get a clearer signal from Anthony's body-mic. She just wished there wasn't a thirty second delay in the feed. Anthony was in an office in the back of the warehouse with Adrianno Martinelli and the unknown silver-haired man. Guards were positioned inside and outside the office door. Billions of dollars in pure cocaine were coming into the port tonight.

Adrianno's son, Ricky, was also returning, after living abroad for years to avoid arrest. The silver-haired man had just identified himself as Lewis Fox, the Godfather of the Dixie Mafia.

Adrianno immediately ordered the two guards to secure Victor.

Anthony sprung forward, slamming into both guards with the full force of his body. His left hand was like rigid steel, smashing against the cartilage of one of the guard's throat, twisting the larynx enough to disable, not to kill.

The guard let out a loud scream of pain and surprise before landing unconscious on the floor. Simultaneously, with his right hand, Anthony aimed with precision and cracked the Beretta against the back of the other guard's head, aiming with precision. The guard slumped to the floor, still and lifeless, but Anthony had lost his gun in the struggle.

He quickly made a run for the door, but it would not open; as he turned, Adrianno dragged a jagged knife across the base of his throat, and blood started trickling down his neck and across his chest.

The silver- haired man aimed a .45 directly at his forehead, and then with one swift movement, Silver Fox cracked him across the skull and in the mouth with the piece, blood spewed everywhere. Adrianno ordered him to kick his gun across the floor.

Silver Fox threw Adrianno a large roll of insulated electrical wire, as he picked up Anthony's Beretta. Working quickly, Silver Fox held the gun on Anthony as Adrianno bound Anthony's hands and feet so that the more he moved the tighter the knots would become. They dragged the semi-conscious Anthony to a chair in front of the huge window overlooking the warehouse.

"He is an impressive specimen," Silver Fox said dispassionately. "Powerful, -- almost like a coiled spring."

Adrianno spun to one side, chuckling. "He is ruthless, isn't he?"

"How long has he worked for you?"

"Four years now, four years of promoting him to run my overseas operations, only to discover from you tonight that he is a damn fed."

"Chase, we have to move in now! Anthony is burnt!" Ashley snapped.

"Roberto and Grayson, get your teams in behind us," barked Chase.

They jumped from the van and up into the bucket truck. Within seconds, the huge piece of machinery was barreling down the narrow curving dirt trail toward the warehouse. The second part of their ground team followed close behind.

"Code Red. Repeat. Code Red. All teams launch immediately." Ashley spoke clearly into the radio, transmitting the message to all parties on the ground, in the sea, and in the air. She continued listening to the audio feed and monitoring the visuals on the screen.

"Oh, my God!" she screamed, flinging the laptop and earpiece to the floor.

"Anthony has been shot by that bastard Fox!"

"Hold the fuck on!" Chase said through clenched teeth as he rammed the truck through the exterior fencing and straight through the front of the building.

Ashley pulled on her bulletproof vest and strapped her AK 47 over her shoulder. "Chase, hurry!" she called over her shoulder as she jumped from the truck and ran toward the back of the warehouse. Bullets were flying by so closely they were whistling in her ears.

Just as they reached the back of the warehouse, four Cartel men scampered down from an overhead ladder. When they thought the last one's feet hit the ground, Chase and Ashley cut them in half with a rush of gunfire. They continued down the corridor to the area closest to the bay.

Ashley swung the weapon over her shoulder, holding the canvas strap to her chest as she climbed the ladder to the second floor. Before she knew it, Grayson was grabbing her and pulling her upward and behind some containers. The night vision goggles were clouding up from perspiration, and she couldn't see well.

Just as Chase was being pulled upward by Roberto, she heard an agonizing scream. Chase had been hit. She tried to go to him, but Grayson would not release his hold on her arm.

They all continued to move slowly toward the end of the corridor in an effort to move Chase to safety and find the room where Anthony was being held. Just around the corner, they saw four gunmen at the end. Roberto took out the two guards on the right, Grayson got the two on the left, and Ashley confronted the one coming in from the dockside.

"Identify yourself and throw your weapon!" she demanded, leveling her .45 straight at his head. His darkly tanned face peered out from under bleached out, expensive cut hair; his sarcastic smirk looked oddly familiar.

"Hey, bitch! Long time no see. I know you missed me," Ricky Martinelli mocked, raising his .45 to her chest.

Heart pounding, Ashley immediately fired, sending a bullet straight through his skull. She watched in horror as the hidden panel door directly behind her opened as she fired her weapon.

"Ricky, my sweet child. You killed my Ricky." Adrianno Martinelli let out a tortured scream. His aim was too quick, too good, and too close; it filled the air with another explosion.

The bullet tore into the Kevlar vest with the impact of a thousand powerful fists; Ashley went down.

More explosions filled the air. Bullets whistled by her ears before splintering chunks out of the wall behind her.

More gunshots followed by steel hitting steel as the rounds went through Adrianno before striking the steel door behind him.

Adrianno was dead; Ricky Martinelli was dead. The Colombian Cartel Drug Lord and his son both lie crumpled on the floor, blood oozing from their lifeless bodies. Ashley vaguely registered Roberto easing Chase down to a kneeling position. Chase needed help, as he was weak from blood loss.

Grayson helped Ashley up and got her inside the darkened room. She looked up and saw Anthony, slumped over in a pool of blood. "Oh my God!" she whispered. "Anthony, Anthony!" She let out an agonizing scream.

*****

"Ashley, Ashley, It's alright." Anthony pulled his wife close into his arms, gently stroking her hair.

"Anthony?" she cried, tears streaming uncontrollably down her face.

"It's okay, baby. I'm right here. You were having a nightmare." Anthony spoke softly, continuing to stroke her hair like he would that of a child.

"Fox killed you," she whispered, shivering all over.

He shifted in the bed, turning onto his side, cupping her face in his palms. "Look at me," he said softly. "Ashley, look at me."

Eventually her gaze returned to meet his, her crystal blue eyes still brimming with tears. A single tear slid down her cheek. He instantly brushed it away, his touch so gentle.

"I can't live without you, Anthony," she choked out. "I tried for four and a half years, and it didn't work. I need you with me; A.J. needs you, too, sweetheart. You can't die."

He stroked her cheek. "I love you, my dear wife, and A. J., my awesome son. I'm not going anywhere. You're both stuck with me. Nothing is going to happen to me."

Sliding closer, he wrapped one arm around her waist. His other arm lifted to stroke her long dark hair. He pushed a few long wayward strands away from her face, and then his mouth came down on hers. His kiss still sent a thrill through her body, sizzling down her spine and settling deep in her core. When his tongue licked at her lips, she whimpered, opening her mouth to grant access.

She ran her fingers through his long dark hair, wrapped her arms around his neck, and pulled him down for a long, hot kiss. Their tongues danced for a second, and then he was sliding into her, stretching her, filling her until she let out a deep moan of pleasure.

"You are perfect." he muttered, spreading her thighs wider with his hot hands. He gave a hard thrust and buried his entire length inside of her, then pressed his mouth to her shoulder, nibbling, and groaned softly.

"It's been too long," she said.

Anthony raised his head and arched his brow. "I was only gone for ten days this time," he teased.

"Ten days is too long!" She ran her fingers over the wet sheen of sweat on his back, closing her eyes and letting the sensations consume her.

"Well, never let it be said that I don't finish what I start."

He started to move again, his pace fast and urgent, then slow and easy, each long thrust bringing her closer to the edge of exploding. His hips started to pivot, driving deeper, hitting a sweet spot that had her moaning uncontrollably.

They moved together in sync. Ripples of release gathered low in her stomach, spreading down toward her thighs and up to her tingling nipples, until they crashed into a passionate wave of emotion that consumed her.

She cried out and buried her face against his solid chest, letting the pleasure take over. As she climaxed, his thrusts grew erratic, unrestrained, and suddenly he shuddered, letting out a hoarse groan.

Finally, Anthony lifted his head and offered a weak smile. "Well, we're obviously still great at doing that!"

A helpless laugh left her throat. "Yeah, we damn sure are."

"Go to sleep, angel." He kissed her on the top of her head, while holding her tight in his arms. "We have a big day tomorrow. The whole gang will be here for my birthday cookout." He flashed white teeth in a sexy grin.

Ashley gave a lazy smile through half-closed lids. They had been through so many crossroads, taken wrong turns, and ended up at dead ends. Fate had corrected their course, bringing their hearts and family back together. She was thankful that they no longer feared what was around the next curve. It had been over a year and, although Fox had not been apprehended, she remained cautious, but felt safe.

Anthony made sure his wife was sleeping peacefully, before easing out of bed and going down the hallway to check on A.J. He sat in an old rocking chair in his son's room just watching him sleep, still unable to believe how much they looked alike. A few minutes later he returned to join his wife in bed and finally drifted off to sleep himself.

Chapter 1

Costa Rica
Saturday

The white blanket of ocean spray crashed up from the rocks of the jetty and appeared suspended, the emerald-blue waters of the Caribbean acting as a backdrop. The spray danced forward and back, positioning itself over thousands of sharp, jagged pieces of rock and shell overlay. It quickly dropped to become ocean again.

Ashley Cameron-Langston walked out on the far edge of the jetty, staring down at the vicious fight between sea and rock.

This desolate section of the Caribbean Northeast Coast of Costa Rica was a small slice of heaven. It was just south of Nicaragua.

A few small villas dotted the coastline, embedded in the gentle sloping mountain face. Two of the larger villas had guest houses that faced the sea. The whole area was densely populated with the largest remaining tropical rainforest in Central America. A. J. loved all the spider monkeys, birds, and giant sea turtles that lived here. He could give you vast amounts of information about them. A. J. knew how fast they grew and how big each one of them would get. His favorite TV show was Animal Planet, at least for this week anyway.

The past year and a half had been a whirlwind of life-altering events. Ashley closed her eyes and lifted her face to the hot sun and warm sea breeze. Ashley opened her eyes and smiled as sunlight sparkled off the marquise diamond on her left hand. She and Anthony had been married for a year and a half now. She still laughed when she thought about how bummed up they all were at the wedding ceremony.

Most of the time they lived here and occasionally visited Florida. Ashley loved their Florida home and missed it, but this was home away from home. They were blessed to have been given the Florida Beach Home. Fox still had not been apprehended so this was the way they had to live.

A. J. had just turned six and adjusted so well. He was his daddy's little man. Anthony still worked for the CIA and was gone often on assignment. Ashley ran the Florida office of her private investigations business and worked as a profiler for the DEA. Her best friends, Gina Rae and Larry, ran the main branch in D.C.

Even though she and Anthony were still in law enforcement, they shielded A. J. from the harsh realities that their careers entailed. The wails of sirens, the whines of ambulances, and the blasts of gunfire were not a part of their tropical paradise.

They tried to make sure that one of them was home with him at all times. On the rare occasions when they both had to be away, A. J. stayed with her aunt and uncle.

And, it was nice to know Aunt Lynn and Uncle Morgan would be their neighbors soon. It had taken over a year for Anthony to heal from the gunshot and knife wounds inflicted by Fox and Martinelli in the last undercover operation two years ago. He had just gone back to work full time and still hurt badly on rainy and damp days.

Suddenly, the silence on the beach was shattered by a dozen simultaneous blasts. Ashley's eyes snapped open and her heart stopped for an instant as she crouched to retrieve her .38 from her ankle strap. She jerked around toward the beach so quickly that she almost lost her footing on the slippery rocks of the jetty. She inhaled deeply and released her breath slowly as the fireworks dropped neon umbrellas of colorful light from the sky. The Fourth of July patrons had started their fireworks early. Ashley watched as a big red macaw took flight across the blue sky, escaping the loud display.

She secured her gun and made her way back to their beach villa, stopping outside to check the huge tent tie-downs to make sure they were securely grounded.

Fifty bamboo Tiki Torches formed a large outer circle around their stone fire pit. The inner circle consisted of tables and chairs with a couple of brightly colored hammocks tied between palm trees. She had labored setting everything up all afternoon.

She had placed six buffet tables underneath the tents, just in case it rained. That was the amazing thing about the tropics; it could be pouring rain one minute and blistering sunshine the next.

Ashley glanced down at her watch; there was barely an hour before their guests would be arriving for Anthony's big birthday bash. She had just enough time to shower and dress. Her Uncle Morgan had just retired as the mayor of D.C. and he and Aunt Lynn had purchased the Palmetto Villa, the last villa down the shoreline. Ashley's cousin, Patrick, and his fiancé, Brease, Chase, Brenda and Craig were all staying with Aunt Lynn and Uncle Morgan.

Roberto, Grayson, Greg, Vince and their wives were all staying at the Palmetto guest villa. Ashley had prepared the downstairs guest room for Gina Rae and Larry. She laughed to herself; it was one big copfest.

Everyone they knew and associated with were cops. Just west of them was the Grand Spa Resort with its warm water creeks and tropical landscaped gardens nestled below the lava rock slopes. DEA Director Madison and CIA Director Jones and their wives had reserved suites there for the whole week. They both had brought their grandchildren and nanny. A. J. would have a five-year-old, two six-year-olds, and an eight-year-old to play with at the party.

Ashley started up the steps to their back deck, dodging Leo as he tore down the steps, chasing a Frisbee, with A. J. in tow.

"Momma. Leo needs a bath." A. J. hollered from the bottom of the steps.

"Why, honey. Does he stink?" She asked.

"No, ma'am. I think he has fleas." A. J. said pulling Leo's ears back and staring down.

"Leo, doesn't have fleas, baby. If you want to go swimming in the ocean, wait a little while and we will all be out here to watch you." She said.

"How did you know I wanted to swim?" He asked.

"Because I'm your mother." Ashley shook her head and stepped up on the back deck.

"Okay, I get to swim later. Leo really doesn't have fleas." A. J. called over his shoulder.

Anthony was busy at the grill, flipping burgers and turning the beef and shrimp kabobs.

She sank right down, her butt landing on the bench with a thud.

She just stared at him, his long hair and strong, high cheekbones below those sexy dark eyes. Her heart did a little jumping jack.

Even after a year and a half of marriage, he still made her melt. They still argued, probably always would as they were both very head strong people.

"Hey, sexy." Anthony winked at her, with a quick lift of his chin.

She stood up, wrapped her arm around his waist, and ran her fingers through his hair, pulling him closer to her.

"I love you." Her voice was heavy with emotion.

"I love you, too." He dipped his head and pressed a tender kiss to her lips. Then he pulled back and said, "I forgot what it was like to have a family.

His smile widened, revealing perfectly white teeth.

"I get it now, why you made the choices you did."

She looked up at him, wiping her tears and her nose on the bottom of his tank top. "I hate that you lost the first years of A.J.'s life."

"We're making up for it now." He said.

Ashley continued to dry her tears and nose on his shirt.

"Hell, you had to go and get all mushy on me didn't you? You're getting soft in your old age, except for snotting on my shirt." Anthony laughed.

A laugh escaped her throat, too, as she slapped Anthony on the butt. "I didn't snot on your shirt. I simply wiped my eyes and nose, and I believe you're older than me, old man."

The sun was beginning to fall from the clear blue sky. It was bright as hell, and Anthony was squinting as he looked down at Ashley. Her face was tanned and radiant; her body covered by a black bikini that rose high on her sleek thighs and barely covered her breasts. She even had a matching ankle strap in black for her gun.

"I'll show you an old man later, sunshine!" He waved the long pronged grill fork at her.

She grinned. "Oh, really? Promises, promises." Ashley jumped out of his reach.

"I'll remember that one. Payback is a bitch." Anthony flashed a half menacing smile.

Barking in the distance caught their attention. Leo had a spider monkey up a palm tree with A. J. rolling in the sand, laughing.

"Leave it to your German Shepherd to tree a monkey!" Anthony laughed.

"Don't pick on Leo; the monkey stole his Frisbee and he wants it back."

"Well, it looks like that monkey will be up the tree for a while." Anthony shook his head.

"I'm going in to shower and change and then I'll be out to help you." She blew him a kiss as she opened the patio door and disappeared inside their villa. She had just walked into their bedroom when her cell phone started ringing.

"Brenda," she said when she heard her friend's voice on the other end of the cell phone.

"Ashley, we're running a little late. Our flight was delayed so it will be about four thirty when we get there."

"Okay, I'm running a little behind too. Just now getting in the shower. I can't wait to see you, Chase and Craig."

"Chase says to have him a drink ready. He's aggravated with airport idiots and Craig said to tell you he's hungry."

"Tell Chase I will have him a double ready and we have mountains of food. We also have a well-stocked liquor cabinet for the adults. And, I made our famous punch. The one you love so much."

"No, you didn't!"

"Sure did. Just be careful about eating all the fruit off the bottom like you did last time or we will bury you in the sand again with just your nose and toes sticking out."

Brenda laughed. "See you soon. Chase is bitching for me to get off the phone so we can get out of this airport."

"Okay, see you guys in a bit." Ashley placed the cell phone back on the nightstand and headed for the shower.

Chapter 2

Ashley walked out onto the patio deck, where some of the party guests were milling around, sipping drinks, and doing Jell-O shots. Everyone had broken up into little groups. The younger ones were on the beach throwing horseshoes, while the older crowd hung out talking and drinking.

She made her way slowly to the farthest corner from the villa and down the steps to the sandy beach below. Hundreds of stars twinkled like diamonds in the dark sky overhead.

The hem of her long flowing white skirt whipped in the breeze above pink platform flip-flops.

They matched perfectly with her pink sequined spaghetti-strap top. Anthony, Chase, and Larry were down at the water's frothy edge, providing a magnificent display of fireworks.

Everyone had eaten and the bonfire was down to a few slow burning embers. It had been a spectacular party so far. The DJ they hired definitely came prepared. He had music covering a fifty year time frame. Everyone had sang and danced to songs from the 60's up to 2014.

"A.J. didn't want to go to bed did he?" Gina asked.

"He never does if there's company here." Ashley said as she plopped down on the corner of the blanket.

Brenda plucked a cherry from the bottom of her glass and popped it in her mouth. "This punch is to die for. You know, it has been a long time since we had this stuff. The last time I acted pretty stupid."

Ashley took a long sip of her frozen margarita. "Oh, but these are better. You haven't been eating the fruit all night, have you?"

"Only half of the night." Brenda giggled.

"I'm with Brenda. The punch is awesome." Gina Rae drained the last of the red liquid from her glass just as Vince walked up carrying a couple of large mouth jugs.

"Refills, anyone? I have punch or margarita." He held up the jugs.

The ladies held their glasses up. "When did you become the designated bartender on the beach?" Ashley asked.

"Oh, when I lost a bet with your husband. I'm your party drink boy instead of water boy." He chuckled.

"I won't even ask what kind of bet you lost."

"Well, don't say I told you but your husbands want to get lucky tonight; they told me to keep the drinks coming.

I told them they shouldn't need the drinks for that, not if they're good husbands…" Vince said in an exaggerated whisper before heading over to the next group.

"Those three act like a bunch of teenagers." Brenda laughed, pointing to their husbands, who were chasing each other up and down the beach with fireworks. They were trying to see who could hold a firecracker the longest before it exploded.

"They are going to blow their damn hands off," Gina Rae said, shaking her head.

"A toast to our three stooges, while they still have all their body parts intact," Ashley replied with a grin as they gently tapped their glasses together.

"And there are definitely some special parts on my man I want to remain intact!" Brenda said in a loud whisper.

"You've definitely had too much to drink, my friend. But, you are so right." Gina said.

"How are the three most beautiful ladies on the coast? Next to my wife, that is…" Morgan knelt down on the blanket and placed his arm around Ashley's shoulders, giving her a hug.

"Great, just watching our husbands act like idiots," Gina Rae replied with a giggle.

"Oh, they're just having fun. Boys will be boys. Even us grown men have to let our hair down sometimes. The ones of us that still have some." He laughed as he ran his hand through his thinning hair.

"You're still the best looking uncle I have and I'm so excited that you and Aunt Lynn are our neighbors now. I couldn't believe it when she told me you bought Palmetto Villa. I mean, just look at this view." Ashley's voice rose with emotion.

"The beach is spectacular here. We still have a lot of unpacking to do. I have more exciting news, though. Patrick is going to be the next D.C. Mayor!" he said.

"Oh my God!"

"Congratulations," Brenda and Gina Rae said in unison.

Morgan kissed Ashley on the cheek. "Lynn, Patrick, and Brease are wiped out so we're going to leave. The party has been great. Tell Anthony 'Happy Birthday' again for us. We'll see you all tomorrow."

"Thanks for coming. I love you." Ashley hugged her uncle good-bye.

Ashley, Gina Rae, and Brenda sipped their drinks and sat on the huge pale blue beach blanket with its pink flamingos embroidered on the edges.

"Do you think you and Anthony will have any more children?" Gina Rae asked.

"I don't know. A.J. is six now. We haven't really talked about having another one. Our jobs keep us really busy."

"I miss having a baby. Craig is all grown up and doesn't need me anymore." Brenda frowned looking down the beach at her eighteen year old son.

"How about you Gina? Are you and Larry going to have kids?" Ashley asked.

Gina Rae flashed her perfect white teeth. "We just started trying."

"Oh my God. Gina Rae, why didn't you tell me?" Ashley squealed.

"That is terrific; you and Larry will be great parents." Brenda said.

"We're pretty excited. I can't wait to have a baby. A little Larry Jr. running around would be great." Gina Rae giggled like a school girl.

"So would a Rae Rae," Brenda added.

"I can just see a prissy little Rae toddling around. You will have plenty of babysitters," Ashley said, patting her friend on the arm.

"I know; it is so exciting. Tonight is the first alcohol I've consumed in months. I'm not pregnant yet but I still want to stay healthy. Once I get pregnant, I won't drink at all. I really don't care if it's a boy or girl, so long as it's healthy."

"I hope you have a better pregnancy than I had. I stayed sick for nine months," Ashley said.

"Chase was a blubbering idiot when I went into labor. We had our drill all planned out. My hospital bag all packed and ready in the hallway closet. My water broke and he jumped out of bed, ran down the stairs, grabbed my bags, and tossed them in the trunk before flying off toward the hospital." Brenda laughed until tears were rolling down her cheeks.

"That sounds precious. What's so funny?" Gina Rae asked.

"He got, he got, ha... halfway, to the hos... hospital, before he re... realized he had left me at h... home," Brenda got out, laughing hysterically.

Ashley and Gina Rae burst out laughing along with her.

"That sounds like Chase." Ashley took another long sip of her margarita.

"Have you thought of any baby names?" Brenda asked Gina Rae.

"We've tossed a few around. If it's a boy, we'll name him after Larry."

"I named A.J. Anthony John after Anthony," Ashley said staring out at the white capping ocean.

"You sound sad," Gina Rae said.

"Just reflecting back. You know, all the things that Anthony missed out on when we were apart. He missed A.J.'s first smile, first words, first steps... he didn't meet him until A. J. was a little over four years old." Ashley frowned.

Gina Rae scooted over close to Ashley and rocked her back and forth, bumping her shoulder against Ashley's.

"He loves you and A.J. so much. His love for you is why he left you to start with… it took me a while to get over wanting to kill him. But what he missed out on is all the more reason for you to have another baby." She smirked.

"I don't know. Sometimes, I don't think we're adult enough to raise A.J. We argue over the most insignificant things.

We're working on talking instead of yelling. He say's I still throw up the past… and I do. I forgave him a long time ago, forgetting just takes a little longer." Ashley admitted.

"Well, hell. Larry and I argue. All couples argue. I don't think that makes us a bad couple or that we'll be bad parents for that matter."

"I agree with Gina. Chase and I argue. We just never do it in front of Craig." Brenda added.

They were all engrossed in girl talk when Leo came charging past their blanket, kicking sand up everywhere.

"Your dog is nuts, Ashley!" Gina Rae said, brushing sand off her legs.

"He is a beautiful Shepherd, but kind of hyper, isn't he?" Brenda asked.

"He's Leo; that's about all I can say.

I guess he finally gave up on the monkey that stole his Frisbee earlier this afternoon," Ashley answered.

"A monkey stole his Frisbee?" Brenda asked.

"Yep, Anthony said only my dog would tree a monkey!"

They all watched as Leo ran up and down the beach.

"What is that in his mouth?" Gina Rae asked. "I don't think it's his Frisbee."

"I don't know. Leo, come!" Ashley commanded. Leo obeyed and came to a quick stop at the edge of their blanket.

"Drop it!" Ashley pointed to the ground.

The three ladies stared down at the small UPS box, chewed on the corners. It was addressed to Ashley at their Florida residence. No postmark, no sender, or return address.

Ashley knelt over and picked up the package by one corner, then rose to her feet.

The package wasn't sealed as Leo had chewed off one corner completely. Ashley stared at the package as if it were a bomb. None of them spoke as she gently lifted the flap and extracted the contents.

Gina Rae noticed that Ashley's hands were shaking, the glow of the full moon illuminating the flicker of apprehension in her eyes.

Ashley slowly lifted a single linen handkerchief from the box. There was no note. Only one letter, a bright red Old English "F" monogrammed dead center, which sent a chill up her spine. Ashley released the offensive piece of cloth and stared as it drifted slowly in the breeze to rest a few feet away in the sand. Trepidation crept up her spine as she lowered her gaze to the handkerchief. "What the hell does this mean?" she asked in a soft, shaky voice.

Gina Rae and Brenda called the guys, who were now running toward them.

Anthony was the first one to reach them and he knelt down beside his wife. "What's wrong, honey?"

All Ashley could do was point. "It's a threat… Fox has found us."

Anthony nodded, a deadly glint filling his eyes as he reached down and lifted the handkerchief up for closer examination. "Yes, I think he has. That has to be the package I threw on the bar when I flew home. I picked our mail up in Florida and then we couldn't find it on the bar the next day. Leo must have taken it; he likes stealing things."

Ashley chewed on her bottom lip, fighting back the tears. "There's no place that's safe anymore. I thought all that shit was far behind us, but I guess it never will be. We've tried to be so careful."

Anthony looked up to see Directors Madison and Jones approaching; Chase had told them what was happening.

Anthony gently placed his hand on Ashley's cheek and she slowly turned away from the water she was staring at. The disappointment and sorrow in her big blue eyes nearly tore him apart.

"Everywhere we go is a risk. Every crossroads we pass through leads back to Jaded Justice." she mumbled almost incoherently before continuing to ramble. "Fox will kill all of us. Turn left, it's there; turn right, it's there…

"You and Brenda get her inside," Larry told Gina Rae as he kissed her on the cheek.

"Vince, stay with the girls. I'll get something to bag the handkerchief and parcel in, although I am sure it will yield no prints and only dog slobber DNA," Chase said, keeping his voice low.

"This is not good," Anthony said.

His eyes strayed to his wife's retreating figure as her friends ushered her into their home.

Once Anthony was sure she was out of hearing range, he turned to his boss.

"What the hell happened?" he demanded, looking straight through Jones.

Director Jones was never the type to waste words or flower things up. "The breach occurred in Florida, the governor's office to be exact. Someone with high security clearance accessed Ashley's file. The only information it contained was relative to the Florida and D.C. operations; there was nothing regarding this location in Costa Rica," he explained, his voice devoid of emotion.

Anthony ran his hands through his hair. "When were you planning to share this information?"

"I didn't acquire the information until this morning. The CIA is conducting the internal investigation now.

I was going to wait until tomorrow, after your birthday celebration, to be the bearer of bad news."

"Why, exactly, does Ashley have a file in the governor's office anyway?" Chase asked.

"She has level five security clearance. It was granted

to her by the governor two years ago when she was conducting investigations for a contractor overseas. This would have been just before she gave part of her business to Gina and Larry and opened the satellite office up in Bay of Sands. And we have an office in the capital building on the third floor," DEA Director Madison answered.

"How detailed is the information that was breached?" Larry questioned.

"Level five security background investigations go back to birth. It would detail your neighbors, friends, relatives, high school, and college.

They would know that she has a son, a home in Bay of Sands, Florida; business interests, vehicle registrations, medical records, every case she has worked, and every court room appearance," Director Madison answered sadly.

"How recent going forward does the file cover?" Anthony demanded.

"Her marriage to you was the last update. Nothing in the file details your Costa Rica home or business ventures here." Jones replied flatly.

"So the last updates would have included Operation Sundown?" Anthony asked.

"The file does include notations from that operation with regards to Adrianno Martinelli and the Colombian Drug Cartel, as well as Lewis Fox and the Dixie Mafia. I'd like to remind everyone that the file was heavily encrypted and, even though access was gained, we don't know that it has been deciphered," Jones stated firmly.

"What the hell is wrong with you people? Why don't you just serve Ash up to the Cartel and Mafia on a silver fucking platter?" Chase growled in disgust.

"Now, calm down, son!" Madison directed.

"Calm down, my ass. She's like my little sister, and the agencies have fucked her over for the last time. You didn't do a good enough job of it last time I guess." Chase stepped to within inches of the face of both directors.

"I agree with Chase. She's my wife. How the fuck could a breach of this magnitude have occurred without some high up authorization? The identity of any undercover agent is strictly confidential," Anthony said, glaring at both Director Jones and Madison.

"Both you boys need to stand down and be rational. Just slow down while we put it all in perspective. Going off half-cocked will get all of you killed." Director Jones attempted to diffuse the situation.

"I don't like any of this shit, but I have to agree with Jones. We need to pull the team together and get them before they get us!" Larry said, stepping solidly between Chase, Anthony, and the directors.

"Jones and I will work through the night and pull an operative team together. We will meet back here, at Anthony's villa later in the morning. In the meantime, the jet is available at the airport. Larry, why don't you go with Chase and take the evidence to our lab? He doesn't need to go alone and get himself in trouble considering his attitude right now."

"I have more questions for Anthony and I'm waiting on a call back from an informant in Florida, which I hope sheds more light on this situation," added Jones.

"Happy fucking birthday, man!" Chase slapped Anthony on the back before joining Larry at the villa to tell the girls bye.

Chapter 3

"It wasn't Fox!"

Ashley blinked at the harsh words and tried to push away the heavy darkness of sleep that covered her. She blinked a few more times, letting her eyes adjust to the bright sunlight streaming through the blinds. The memories came flooding back. She had cried herself to sleep. Gina Rae and Brenda had sat on the foot of the bed until she'd drifted off. She glanced over at the clock; it was two thirty in the afternoon. *Oh, my God. I slept for over fourteen hours.*

She pulled the blanket closer, suddenly feeling chilled and a little disoriented. "What are you talking about?"

Anthony sat on the bed, his leg brushing her thigh.

"It wasn't Fox who sent the package to our home in Bay City.

Chase and Larry flew the evidence to the lab around two this morning. They just called with the results a couple of hours ago. Brenda is headed to pick them up at the airstrip now."

Ashley scrambled into a sitting position. Okay, maybe things were not as bad as she'd thought. "It wasn't Fox? Are you sure?" she asked.

Anthony shook his head slowly. "It's impossible, but the only DNA on the seal of the package, other than Leo's dog slobber; belongs to Ricky Martinelli."

Her heart slammed into her ribs. "That's impossible; he's dead. I killed him over a year ago." She ran a hand through her hair.

"Oh, my God! Where's A. J.?" she asked, panic-stricken.

The faint lines around Anthony's mouth deepened. "He's fine, but it gets worse. There's a price on your head. Damn high, too."

"So you're telling me that two people want me dead? The sender of the package and someone else?" She tried to swallow, but it felt like she was swallowing shards of glass.

"I'll be with you and A. J. Don't worry. You'll both be safe." Anthony's fingers were caressing her arms, moving in small, light strokes against her skin.

"How can you be so sure it isn't Fox?" Ashley asked, still confused.

"Nothing we have found leads to Fox. The team is all pulling together, authorized by both Directors Jones and Madison. There is a leak at the governor's office. They're going to find out who accessed the files." He exhaled a very rough breath, but didn't release her.

Easy for him to say.

He wasn't the one being targeted by two killers, one probably Mafia and the other Colombian Drug Cartel. She stared into her husband's eyes. He had been targeted for death many times. She knew it. Death was his life. His job. He was a fighter and a survivor, so was she.

"I refuse to be helpless. I never have been and I won't start now!" She pushed the covers away; she wore a loose T-shirt and a pair of jogging shorts. Not exactly sexy, but Anthony's gaze still dropped to her long legs, and lingered. Her heart beat faster. "We have to protect A. J. I'm assuming the breach in security occurred in the States, correct?" He stood as she paced back and forth.

His gaze wasn't on her legs anymore. That too intense stare raked her pain-stricken face.

"Correct."

"How the hell could the package have contained Ricky Martinelli's DNA?" she asked.

"I don't have an answer to that one yet. They ran it three times and it came back the same match every time." Anthony shook his head.

"None of this makes any sense!" Ashley muttered.

"No, it doesn't."

"Okay. I'll check with Uncle Morgan and Aunt Lynn about keeping A. J. and looking after our place here. They're just next door and I am sure they won't mind. We're going back to Florida." Her voice was firm and uncompromising.

It was his turn to run his hands through his hair.

"No. I'm going with the team, but you'll stay here."

Ashley dropped her gaze from Anthony's face to his bare chest, ripped with muscles. She stared at the Indian tattoo a few inches wide that covered his heart. The dark black ink formed jagged swords positioned in the pattern of a wolf howling at a red moon.

"I'll always stand between you and any person who comes after you and A. J.," he said.

She believed him, but Anthony was flesh and blood. No matter how invincible he thought he was, he couldn't stop bullets. He could die, too. Then what would happen? I'd be without him again, and so would A. J.

She pulled her bottom lip between her teeth, hesitated, and then said, "I'm going to the States. If I don't, they'll keep looking for me and I will not lead them here to A. J.," she said quietly.

Anthony took a deep breath and huffed it out. He'd done everything possible to keep her safe and alive. He'd given her up. That had been everything. "Don't push me on this."

"I don't want to spend the rest of my life running or looking over my shoulder." She kept her voice calm with an effort.

Anthony knew people who had spent years running.

That life – it sucked. Always looking over your shoulder and never letting your guard down... But, there was something else she needed to understand before she made this decision and he could only relay a portion of the information at this time.

"Jones is worried about the leak at the governor's office in Florida, and Madison is afraid his DEA operatives have all been compromised as well. That means Chase and Brenda aren't safe, either. Chase went off on all of them last night. Both Jones and Madison have authorized full team participation. But it is strictly under the radar, off the record. We will be the equivalent of mercenaries. We'll have access to all the equipment, weapons, and intel necessary, but officially this operation will not exist."

He could see the struggle in Ashley's face.

"No hiding." She gave a slow nod.

"That's not ... that's not the way I want us to live. I don't want to be afraid, every day, that the Cartel or Mafia is coming after me or my family. I want A. J. to grow up living a normal life."

Anthony stared down at her. *Does she realize how strong she truly is?* he wondered.

"I want to go after him. I want Fox and whoever they are to fear! We will be the hunters, not the hunted." She swallowed and exhaled slowly.

His hands were clenched so tightly that his knuckles ached. His teeth ground together, but against his better judgment, he managed to say, "I'm lead on this team. You have to follow orders. When it comes to keeping you alive, I'm the one in charge. I'm the one who is going to stand between you and Hell."

His gaze continued to search hers. "You might not like me. Hell, you might hate me before it's over, but too bad. This isn't about emotion. It has to be about getting the job done. I still don't want you going on this operation, but I see arguing with you would be pointless."

Her jaw clenched as she stood toe to toe with him. She didn't want to get used to any of this, and Anthony was stripping away all of her choices. "There is nothing to argue about, I'm part of the team."

"Why can't you just let me handle it? You need to stay here with A.J."

"Let you handle it… like you did before and run off with no explanation!" Ashley said loudly.

"Go ahead and throw up that shit, why don't you. You don't trust me." Anthony said louder.

"It's not about trust, you asshole. I was an officer before I met you and a damn good one."

"I know you're a damn good cop. That's not the point. You're my wife too, you know. I think it's natural for me to feel the way I do."

"Our relationship as husband and wife don't come into this…" Ashley said frankly.

"So, you don't think you can… Trust yourself around me…" he said with a slow, sexy grin, trying to release the tension in the air. It worked. Ashley couldn't help but lighten up.

"You're an ass, but the man I love." Her lashes swept up. "I've lost too much time with my husband already. We will do this operation your way and it will be our last." Her left hand lifted and pressed lightly against the line of his jaw. "We retire after this."

He kissed her. His mouth took hers, rough, hungry, because he couldn't hold back. He needed her too much; he always had. The pain of the past years… Being without her… It didn't matter anymore. She was with him now, in his arms. He pulled her even closer. She stumbled against the bed and laughed against his lips. That laugh was the sweetest sound he knew. He would spend the rest of his life making her happy. He wanted forever with her. If this meant making changes, then so be it…

"Yes, sweetheart, we retire after this operation," Anthony promised as they became lost in each other's arms.

Chapter 4

Ashley walked across the plush carpeting of their master bedroom, and opened the bathroom door. She glanced down at the faint red marks around her wrists and upper arms, evidence of their passionate lovemaking. Anthony didn't know his own strength; she would have bruises tomorrow. The pulsating jets of hot water brought life back into her limbs. She rinsed the last of the gardenia scented suds from her body and stepped out of the shower, reaching for a large fluffy towel. Flipping her head over, she dried her thick mass of long dark hair before patting her body dry. In this humidity, it didn't take long to dry off.

She decided not to straighten her hair and just sprayed it with a little detangler.

She wiped down the steamed-up mirror and stared at the too-pale face, her wide blue eyes all puffy from crying last night and her wet unruly hair. *"Who are you and what have you done with me?"*

Ashley didn't wait for an answer from herself. She pulled a red tank top over her head, pulled on cut-off jean shorts, and slipped her feet into a pair of red flip-flops. Taking another breath, she pulled herself together and walked out of the bathroom, closing the door behind her and heading for the stairs.

"Good evening, sleepyhead," Gina Rae said as Ashley descended the stairs.

"Morning, or should I say afternoon. I can't believe I slept the day away," she said quietly.

"It's okay; you needed the rest. Is there something I can help you with or get for you?"

Ashley flushed. "I…. no…. that is, I don't know."

She clutched the breakfast bar, her knuckles white from the death grip she had on the edge.

"I just can't believe it's starting all over again!"

Gina Rae hadn't seen Ashley this distraught since Anthony almost died in Operation Sundown. She knew her best friend still suffered from horrible nightmares occasionally, but she refused to take medication to help her sleep. "I am so sorry. They will get the damned…." The sound of the front door opened, killing the rest of her words.

Chase, Larry, and Brenda walked in; Chase and Larry looked like they hadn't slept in a month.

"Sweetie, you okay?" Brenda asked as she took the vacant chair across from where Ashley stood at the breakfast bar.

Ashley's throat went dry. She swallowed a few times, bringing much needed moisture to her mouth and something indefinable flickered across her face.

"I'm fine." She fought the tears that pricked at her eyelids. It took a serious amount of willpower to blink them back. She refused to cry, she absolutely refused to cry.

"I'm sorry our reunion for Anthony's birthday turned to crap last night and that I went to pieces on all of you," she said, her voice trembling. Averting her eyes for a moment, she studied the oil seascape painting handing on the wall opposite the breakfast table. She had painted it their second month here; it reminded her of peace and hope.

"It's okay, honey. Don't give it another thought." Brenda shook her head.

"Besides, we are all family. What happens to one of us happens to all of us," Gina Rae said, patting Ashley's hand.

"What did you find out?" Ashley asked Chase.

"I don't know how much Anthony has already told you, but the DNA on the seal of the package came back to Ricky Martinelli."

"He told me. That's just not possible."

Chase nodded, a deadly glint filling his eyes.

"Yeah, I thought so at first, but DNA doesn't lie and the seal wasn't tampered with; you know… not sealed, unsealed, and resealed years later."

"Who do you think sent it?" She asked as she turned to watch Anthony coming up on the back deck from the beach.

"I'm assuming there is a connection to the hit taken out on you."

Ice filled her veins. "You think they'll come after me?"

"What do you think?"

"I think we have to get the bastards first," she replied stiffly.

Anthony walked across the kitchen and returned to his wife's side, shoving a fizzing soda in her hand.

"Thanks." She smiled at him and took a long sip, letting the cold liquid slide down her throat.

"Oh, caffeine, how could I live without you?"

"You need to cut down. You drink way too much soda." Anthony cracked a genuine smile.

She patted the stool next to her for Anthony to sit, still sipping sway. "Maybe, one day."

Chase stared across the table, unable to get any words out. He felt his brain working, spinning in circles, circuits overheating, sparks igniting. They had to focus and plan a course of action.

Brenda kissed her husband on the cheek. "Gina Rae and I are going to walk down the beach and check on A. J. We'll leave you guys to talk." They each gave Ashley a quick hug and headed out the door.

As soon as the door closed, Larry radioed Vince to escort the girls over to Morgan and Lynn's. A few minutes later Roberto and Grayson entered, followed shortly by Directors Madison and Jones.

"This is the line of work that we have chosen," said Director Jones gently.

"Our responsibility to justice supersedes all bonds of kinship and affection. It is eternal. I wish it were otherwise. In my career, I've had to kill one and arrest three of my own men. Good men... gone bad. I live with that every day. But I'd do it again in a heartbeat. Now there is another leak, another man gone bad. We don't know their identity yet. Almost two years ago we successfully brought about the downfall of the Dixie Mafia and the Colombian Drug Cartel. We managed to take out the Cartel leaders by killing Adrianno Martinelli and his son, Ricky. Fox is still at large and has remained elusive to capture. Last night, confidential informants provided detailed information regarding a contract hit, the target being Ashley Cameron-Langston."

"What is the price on her head?" Anthony asked solemnly.

Rumor is on the street that it is the highest dollar hit in my twenty-five years. I can't release the figure until I have more verification. It is not confirmed that the package received is in any way connected to this contract hit, as the DNA from the package is that of a dead man, Ricky Martinelli. This places us in a precarious situation."

"Precarious... that's an understatement." Chase said.

"I agree. A high dollar price tag is on my wife's head and you don't have a clue who is backing the hit?

Come, on now. All of us have been around long enough to know there are only a handful of organizations capable of fronting that kind of money for a hit." Anthony snorted in disgust.

"It's either the Colombian's or the Dixie Mafia." Chase replied.

"By precarious, I mean we go off the radar so to speak." Jones said quietly.

"The whole team, right?" Anthony asked.
Director Jones swallowed hard before continuing.

"Yes. The CIA is currently investigating the leak in the governor's office. That being said, Director Madison and I agree this operation will have to be covert. You will have all the same team members you had in Operation Sundown for this operation. We will work from remote locations; safe houses and covert buildings. Madison and I will be your only contacts. Outside of this sector, the operation does not exist. All of the team will fly out for Florida in two days."

Director Madison added, "I'll be assigning men here to watch over the family members staying behind. I believe that your wife and son can stay for an extended period of time, is that right?"

"Yes, they can." Chase answered.

My understanding is that you begin testifying in a federal trial in D.C. next week and that Gina Rae must return to handle some open on-going investigations?" Madison looked at Larry.

"Yes, sir." Larry nodded his head.

"Patrick must return to D.C. His fiancé, Brease, is CIA and will be part of our team. Jones is there anything I have missed?"

"I don't think so… We will be doing everything possible to ensure the safety of all family and team members. This will be Operation Crossroads, as it can go many directions or end up at a dead-end quickly. We will all meet at the abandoned airport on County Line Road just outside of Bay City at seven a.m. sharp in three days. I'm leaving this afternoon with my family and returning to Florida to prep for this operation, as is Director Madison."

"I know that I do not need to remind any of you that this is a very covert operation. Trust no-one outside of our immediate team. You must use precautionary measures any time you come and go, any time you have conversations with each other on cell or landlines," Madison said in closing.

"Will we be provided with all intel obtained from informants when we meet in three days?" Ashley asked.

"Absolutely, why would you not?" Jones said.

"No reason. Just wanted to make sure there are no last minute surprises." Ashley said.

"If there are no further questions at this time, we will be leaving. Take the next couple of days to spend with your families and get your affairs in order. This may be a very long operation," Madison said regretfully.

Ashley, Anthony, Chase, and Larry stood staring out the glass patio doors at the white capping ocean waves as the Directors left the villa.

Chapter 5

Costa Rica
Monday

The mid-day sun had almost reached its peak directly overhead. A few storm clouds still lingered high in the sky. Ashley, Anthony, and A.J. had come out to play volleyball over an hour ago. They always brought A.J. out to the beach early in the day as the noon sun was extremely hot.

"Our ball. Our ball. You missed, Daddy. You hit the net, it's our point too." A.J. hollered.

"Here you go, buddy," Anthony said as he rolled the ball under the net to his son.

"Toss it up, and I'll spike it down," Ashley said.
"Hey, that's no fair. It's already two against one," Anthony complained.

"No, it's not. You have Leo." She laughed as she spiked the ball over the net. Leo immediately ran over, barking, and wrapped his paws around the ball.

"Yeah, he's a good partner. He holds the ball to keep me from getting it, and when he finally gives it up...." Anthony laughed as he coaxed the ball away from Leo and held it up. "It's dripping with dog slobber."

"He's just getting it clean for you, daddy."

"So clean I can't hold onto it." Anthony said dropping the ball again.

Ashley felt a few drops hit her arm and glanced up to see that the clouds had finally decided to empty. It was drizzling very lightly. In Costa Rica it was a common occurrence for it to rain hard one second and be shining brightly the next. "Everybody run for the house."

They ran, with Leo close on their heels, up the sandy path to their back deck. Ashley slid the patio door open just as Leo ran past, almost knocking her off her feet.

Anthony swept her up in his arms, laughing as he slid the door closed behind them.

"Looks like we made it inside just in time," she said, staring out the door at the rain pouring down.

"It will pass quickly."

She smiled one of those smiles that really got to him, the kind of smile that could be seen in her eyes and came straight from the heart.

"You can put me down now."

He slid her down the length of his body until her feet hit the floor. "Did you have a good time today?"

"Yes, I had a great time. I got to spend it with my two favorite men."

"I'm a man, Momma," A.J. said.

"Yes, you are. My little man…" Her heart swelled as she brushed the hair back from her son's face. She didn't want the day to end but it kept edging its way forward.

"I wish we could just stop time right here," she murmured, lingering by the door.

Anthony leaned his hand on the wall just above her head, creating intimacy out of the space in the hall. "Yeah, I know." He stared down at A.J. as he made Leo sit before giving him dog treats.

"I'm hungry," A.J. said.

Anthony reached down and swept up his son, twirling him in the air, before swinging him up on top of his shoulders. "How about we all get cleaned up and go out for pizza?"

"Yeah, yeah. I want pepperoni pizza." A.J. said as he looked down at his mom.

"Ruff, ruff, ruff." Leo barked loudly, circling Anthony.

"It's okay, Leo. We'll bring you back some pizza bones," Ashley said, scratching him behind the ears.

"Leo doesn't want anybody messing with his buddy." Anthony said as he sat A. J. back down.

Twenty minutes later, she came downstairs changed into a white tank top and jeans. She could hear Anthony and A.J. upstairs singing, "When She Says Baby." She stared out the window. A beautiful double rainbow spread its pastel colors across the eastern sky.

"You guys hurry up. You have to see this," she called out.

A.J. came running down the stairs. "What? What?"

Ashley pointed out the patio doors. "Look, right over there, baby."

"It's two rainbows. Wow. That's pretty. That's the first time I've seen two of them together. There really isn't a pot of gold at the end, you know." he asked.

"That's what they say, honey." Ashley thought how advanced A. J. was for his years.

"What are you oohing about?" Anthony asked as he entered the living room.

"Look, Daddy. Look at the rainbows."

"It sure is pretty, son." Anthony looked out at the wide pastel display of colors painting the sky.

"Mommy, you and Daddy are twins." A.J. laughed.

"What are you talking about, honey?" she asked.

"You're dressed alike."

Anthony looked down at his white tank top and jeans and then looked over at Ashley and laughed. "Great minds think alike."

Ashley wrapped her arm around Anthony's waist. "They sure do."

Anthony grabbed the keys off the bar. "Let's go get pizza. No arguing this time about who sits with their back to the door."

"Who does that? Certainly not me." Ashley said.

"No, certainly not you." Anthony smirked.

****

The sun had long since set when the Langton family returned home. An afternoon of pizza, arcades, and a trip to the zoo had worn them all out. Anthony pulled into the garage and got out to get their sleeping son. He tossed the keys to Ashley. "I'll bring him in, he's exhausted. Just unlock the door."

She entered the passcode to the alarm and held the door open for her husband and son. Much later, Ashley and Anthony lay in bed with the moonlight casting a silver glow across them.

"You okay?" he murmured softly.

"Hmm." She felt scared. And without her realizing it, the tears came silently sliding down her cheeks.

Anthony sensed her tears. He hated seeing her cry. She was so strong and she very seldom broke down, so he was at a loss as to what to do as she had cried more the past week than the whole time he had known her. He took her into his arms.

At first she fought him, fought against the feeling of wanting to collapse there and just cling to him. "I don't cry. I hate this feeling and I hate this fucking shit. Once again, our lives our disrupted by the fucking Mafia or Cartel." Ashley fought the tears.

"It's okay. Baby." Anthony said.

"What if they get to A. J. or you… trying to take me out?"

"I won't let that happen."

Surrendering, she wrapped her arms around his neck and just allowed the sobs to come. They wracked her body. She was always so strong, but this time it was a welcome release.

Anthony held her for a long time, stroking her hair, whispering that everything would be all right.

Finally, Ashley raised her head from his chest and looked up at him. "I'm sorry. I just want all this to be over. I don't want to ever have to leave A.J. like this again. I hate that bastard Fox for doing this to my family. No more tears. I will rip his fucking head off." She said automatically stiffening her back very straight.

"Don't worry. We can handle this, we always do." he assured her.

"I know we can do anything; I'm just tired of having to."

He looked down at her tear-stained face and began wiping away the telltale tracks with his thumb. He brought his mouth down gently on hers and kissed her, hoping he could reassure her and make her realize that, before he'd allow anything to happen to her, he'd give up his life.

Chapter 6

Anthony woke slowly, aching all over, his head throbbing. He was sitting in a recliner seat in a mid-size, luxurious executive jet, a blanket over him, and a plump pillow behind his head. The windows were darkened; the noise and vibrations indicated that they were still in flight. It was only a three and a half hour flight, but none of them had slept much in the past two days. He glanced at the lighted dial of his Rolex; they had been in flight for two hours. The directors had felt that leaving Costa Rica in the middle of the night, under the cover of darkness, was safest. No chances were being taken. The jet was going to land at the old abandoned airport. With the hour time differential, they would be on time for the morning meeting. With the progress they were making, they would be about forty-five minutes early.

Anthony looked around; his wife and the rest of the team were in the cabin. He and Ashley had spent the past two days with A. J. Both of them hated to leave him, but they knew he would be safe with Morgan and Lynn. He was thinking about the operation when movement in the wide leather couch across the aisle caught his eye.

Ashley looked up and gave a slight yawn. "Where are we?"

"Halfway across the Gulf by now, I imagine."

She stared at her husband, who was now stretching his long legs and rotating his shoulders. It was still hard for him to sit for long periods of time. The gunshot and knife wounds had taken a toll on his body. She shuddered remembering that one of the bullets had barely missed his femoral artery. The re-used bullets Fox had taken from slain officers, thanks to the medical examiner he had bought.

"Are you cold?" he asked, noticing her shiver.

She swallowed. "No, just remembering the last operation. You almost died."

"You came very close as well." Tony stated sternly.

"I know." She said quietly.

The fear crawling around in his chest made his lips tighten. Damn it. This was precisely why he'd originally told her she wasn't coming. He didn't want to worry about Ashley. Because of her impulsive nature, he'd done a lot of worrying when they were together, always on edge when she took on a particularly risky assignment. She always chased the heavy hitters, the ones who sent her headfirst into life-threatening situations. In her opinion, those were the ones that made a difference. He knew a part of it had to do with proving herself, in the beginning. There were few female narcotic agents. So she took risks. Most of the time they paid off. Other times…

Anthony was suddenly tempted to reach across the seat and shake some sense into her. His anger had built up over the past twenty four hours. He simply did not want her going on this operation. He had a bad feeling about all of it.

"Why did you insist on doing this operation?" he burst out. "I told you I didn't think it was a good idea, that your safety was at risk and instead of listening, you charge into the situation blindly like a bull after a damn red flag. You don't ever listen to me. I worked side by side with the

Cartel for years, if you recall. They will do anything when they have a vendetta against someone. Dammit, Ashley, they would have killed your cousin had I not been the undercover operative the hit was handed off to. And it's not just the Colombian's... The Dixie Mafia as well.

Anthony continued to rant, not giving her a chance to speak. "And we both know what Fox is capable of doing. Every time I look in the mirror, I have the scars to remind me, so do you." He said.

"I know, Anthony."

"I walked away from you a long time ago so it would never come to this shit. A contract hit. Are you really so damn blind?" He shook his head in bewilderment and anger.

She seemed unperturbed. "I'm not blind to any situation, but I refuse to run and hide in fear." She raised one dark brown eyebrow. And don't tell me you wouldn't feel the same way if it were you with the contract on your head."

"Yeah, so? I'm your husband. You should have stayed home where I could have ensured your safety," he grumbled.

"I'm a cop, remember? I'm not going to run and hide and wait for them to take out my son." She snapped.

"You're being a stubborn ass."

"You're acting like an egotistical jerk. And don't forget you were a pretty sorry asshole before you ever left for your undercover operation in the first place. That last month, five out of seven nights you were in a bar drunk!" Sucking in a breath, she stared at him. She couldn't believe she had stooped to the level of throwing the past in his face.

"Well, if you had put me before your damn job, maybe I would have stayed home more!" Anthony barked.

"That is frigging priceless coming from you! I guess I never told you the day I came home and found your lengthy eighteen-word note saying you were fucking gone that I had given notice that morning." Ashley bit back.

"You're acting like a bitch. Why didn't you tell me or try to get in touch with me?"

"You're a fucking prick. Why should I have? I had our son to take care of… alone. Almost five years without a damn word, Anthony. I thought you were dead. You made it really clear that you had moved on… told me to go on with my life, remember."

"I wondered how long it would take for you to go there. Almost two years. We've been married a year and a half now. Maybe I resent losing the first four years of my only son's life. Have you felt this way the whole damn time? I left to protect the only thing I had ever loved at that time…YOU"

"I married you because I love you. I forgave you a long time ago; forgetting takes time." she said.

"Well, I can't change a damn thing," he muttered.

"Neither can I. Listen, I know you're concerned about me. Scared for me…. You have to quit going off like this." She trailed off suddenly, slightly frazzled.

He sighed. "You just don't want to believe this is a suicide mission. It is you know… a pure damn suicide mission."

"We will find the bastards and kill them, it's that simple. Our team is the best there is and you know it. You won't find any better anywhere; we all know how each other thinks and how to react to one another. We have all worked together for years, except for when you decided to abandon all of us at the DEA and go solo with the CIA for years." She could have cut her tongue out the minute the words escaped her lips.

"Why don't you just throw up all the shit from the past? I mean it's not like I just ran off for no reason. You had a damn hit on your stupid ass head then, too!" He practically snarled the words.

Her perceptive blue eyes studied him again. For a few long moments, their gazes locked in heated disagreement, until Ashley finally shook her head and broke the eye contact. "I don't expect you to understand."

Anthony didn't like her sudden lack of expression, or the dull note to her voice, but he wasn't going to push her on the issue right now. He knew from past experience that, when pushed too far, she was capable of completely shutting down, becoming detached, cold and robotic.

She would absorb herself in an operation and then there would be nothing left of her but a shell afterwards.

Sometimes he wondered if he could ever make up for all the mistakes he had made. It was really ironic, they both loved their jobs to a degree; yet their work was always the source of their fights.

The sound of the partition door opening behind them caught both their attention. Chase stepped through and plopped down in the seat on the opposite side of the couch.

"How close are we?" he asked, peering out the octagonal window into the dark night.

"What is it with you two?" Anthony said. "You and Ash ask the same thing the minute you wake up. Are we there yet? Are we there yet? You two sound like a couple of parrots. In answer to your question, we should be landing in about an hour and a half."

"I couldn't sleep. Roberto and Grayson both snore!"

"So does Ashley." Anthony said.

Chase glanced over at Ashley. From the look on her face, he knew they were still arguing about her being part of this operation. She was like his little sister, but he also understood Anthony's point of view. Hopefully, they would both get it together; now was not the time for relationship issues to surface and compromise the operation. They needed all their wits about them to handle this one.

"Why the hell did the directors want to meet at seven in the morning anyway?" Chase asked.

"I think they were looking at getting us there during the hours of darkness. Less conspicuous, and safer. This way it's harder for anyone to follow us." Anthony answered.

"Well, this was supposed to be our vacation. I mean it's not like we couldn't have started later in the day!" Chase grumbled.

"I agree. I have always preferred working nights and sleeping in late the next day. But, it is what it is. You want some coffee?" Anthony asked.

"Yeah, I'll have a cup. May as well get the day started out right with a shot of caffeine." Chase said, rubbing his eyes and noting that Ashley had yet to speak a word to either of them. Anthony must have really pissed her off.

The remainder of the flight was somber. And silent. Deathly silent. Ashley kept her gaze glued to the window for most of it, unable to look at Anthony for fear she'd say something else she would bitterly regret.

Chapter 7

Ashley felt butterflies in her stomach as the plane started to descend. The sudden decrease in altitude had her ears popping. She sat up straight with a death grip on the handles beside her. Within seconds, the engine sound died to a purr. When Ashley heard the skidding of the plane tires bumping the old paved runway, she released her breath. She hadn't liked flying since the twin engine Cessna she was in crashed. She was a spotter, flying over a field of dope when the plane malfunctioned. The pilot had to put her down quickly, landing in a field full of cows. Amazingly enough they both walked away from the crash with no injuries. It just made her dread all plane trips, she didn't breathe easy until they landed safely.

The old airport building slowly moved across the window as the plane coasted to a rest on the runway closest to the back entrance to the building. Its big windows still looked long and sad, just like she remembered them from their last operation. Roberto and Grayson were opening the door and dropping the stairs when she looked up and saw Anthony staring down at her with an unreadable expression. He quickly turned away and exited the plane.

"Let's get this show on the road," Chase said.

Ashley grabbed her bag, slipped her feet back into her sandals, and climbed down the stairs. The minute the faint sea breeze hit her face, she felt like she was back home. It was going to be a scorcher if the heat at 6:45 a.m. was any indication of the weather for later in the day. She looked down at her tattered faded jeans and black tank top, thinking she had chosen her wardrobe wisely.

"We will get those bastards, don't you worry," Brease said as she walked up beside Ashley.

"I know. Is Patrick okay with you working this operation?" she asked.

Brease gave a short laugh. "He knew I was CIA when we became engaged. He understands what my job entails."

Ashley looked down at the petite blonde, blue-eyed Brease with a knowing smile. "I know Patrick loves you and he's a very patient and compassionate man. Just don't ever let your jobs come between the two of you. Always try to remember, the job is what you do, not who you are…"

Roberto and Grayson, with Vince in tow, passed through the airport's unremarkable looking lobby ahead of the girls and descended the stairs leading to the conference room.

Just outside the door, four heavily armored guards were positioned.

There were two on either side of the door. Ashley glanced down the hall, noting another set of four guards.

Inside the conference room on the smooth white painted walls were mounted a pair of large, flat plasma display monitors. Madison and Jones took their seats at a table of brushed steel in the front of the room. Anthony sat at the adjacent table in front of the room as well, looking through a stack of files. As soon as everyone was seated,

Jones began to speak without ceremony.

"We have spent quite a large sum of money updating the security here at our new offices. All the windows have been equipped with an oscillator material, rendering any attempt at laser or acoustic surveillance from the outside virtually impossible. A cone of radio waves constantly surrounds the building, preventing all forms of electronic eavesdropping.

These waves will disable cell phones, making them useless in the building. There is an access panel located behind here."

He pointed to the large painting on the wall. "Should an emergency arise; Madison, Anthony, and I have the only access keys to deactivate the security system, as well as the adjacent vault containing every arsenal weapon imaginable. Everything we say in this room is strictly confidential and needs to remain among team members only. Is that understood?" he asked looking across the room at every member seated.

Once he was satisfied that the confidentiality clause was clearly understood, he continued.

"We have obtained additional information from a confidential informant regarding the contract hit on Agent Ashley Cameron. Excuse me, it's now Ashley Langston." Director Jones gave her a slight apologetic smile.

"We arrested several arms dealers yesterday morning. The interesting thing about their arrest is that two of them were Dixie Mafia and three were Colombian Drug Cartel members. I don't have to tell you that it's uncommon for two separate organized crime groups to work together on any venture. Especially the Dixie Mafia and the Colombian Cartel, they have been rivals for years. We were able to get one of them to talk. Oaths tend to loosen their holds when money changes hands, and I do mean serious money," Jones said with a sardonic smile.

"Now, you've really lost me. Why would the CIA be paying Mafia and Cartel thugs for information?" Chase asked, bewildered.

"I never said we paid the organized crime thugs. I said money changed hands. Mercenaries, ex-CIA were hired for interrogation purposes. Ten hours on a scopolamine drip, six hours in a padded crypt with screeching sounds blaring through a sound system, and ending with a bullet to each knee cap. Whatever it took to break one of them, the interrogators were all too willing to do." Jones said without emotion.

Utter stillness settled around Ashley. All she could hear was the sound of her own breathing, magnified a dozen times in her ears, and the rapid thud of her heartbeat. Previous operations over the past fourteen years had never utilized such brutal means of extracting information. She couldn't shake the question of why now. Ashley looked imploringly over at Chase, she knew the answer.

"I see the bewilderment on each of your faces," Jones said. "The one question you are probably asking yourself is… what kind of price would have to be on Mrs. Ashley Langston's head for us to resort to such measures? It is one of the highest I have ever seen, one-million dollars… in cash!"

"Do you have any idea how many takers there will be on a contract hit with such a high dollar amount?" Madison asked, standing from behind the steel table.

"One million dollars?" Ashley asked in a hoarse, unrecognizable voice. Now she knew why Anthony was so adamant that she stay in Costa Rica. With that price on her head, she might not walk away from this one alive. She would never see Anthony again; never see A. J. grow up… Bile nearly gagged her. Anthony knew, he knew it was a million dollar hit. That's why he was such an ass and didn't want her being a part of this operation.

Even Chase had seemed a little shell-shocked.

"We'll get them first, Ash." He said trying to convince himself or Ashley, Chase wasn't sure.

"Okay." A multitude of emotions swirled inside her. She couldn't believe this was happening all over again. The last operation was a living nightmare.

The next four hours were spent reviewing slide after slide of Mafia and Cartel henchmen and their last known locations. A short bio on each member defined their specialties, from drug and gun trafficking to demolition and explosive experts. The long list of assassins on both payrolls was saved for last.

"Let's take a quick lunch break, we have to contact the interrogation team and see what additional information they may have obtained. We will return in one hour. Food has been catered in downstairs at the old airport café." Madison announced, sensing the rising emotion in the room.

An hour later everyone filed back into the conference room and took a seat.

"Let's take a look at what we know." Jones commanded everyone's attention, ready to get back on task.

"Here are the autopsy photos and reports on Ricky Martinelli and Adrianno Martinelli. They are both dead, as you can see." Jones pushed the buttons on the small black remote control he held in his hand. One of the plasma screens dissolved into another image, followed by another and another. *Those two looked much better dead*, Ashley said to herself.

"Based on newly gained information, the death of these two men, one or both, we are not sure…. seems to be the source for the contract hit on Agent Langston."

"How are the deaths of these men the source of the hit on Ashley? Both father and son are dead. Fox has no loyalty to anyone. His only reason for retaliation would be the loss of his drug cargo in the last operation. He doesn't have a personal interest in this, except the federal seizure of his assets through the RICO Act." Chase stated.

"Let me see if I can take the evidence and information we have and explain a possible motive." Jones continued with more and more information. More and more screens flashed with photos and reports on FBI Director Lawrence from the last operation. The next screen was the suicide note written by Lawrence. Highlighted portions included him being on the Martinelli payroll and being owned by the Dixie Mafia. Also highlighted was the killing of the boxer whom Fox's wife, Donna, had an affair. Fox had had him killed. Highlighted and double underlined was the section Lawrence had detailed about the linen handkerchief found shoved down the boxer's throat after he was stabbed twenty-six times. The handkerchief had an Old English monogrammed "F," just like the one Ashley had received.

"We believe the connection or tie between the two crime families was FBI Director Lawrence. Since he committed suicide, we are left with his wife and daughter." Jones cleared his throat before continuing.

His daughter is Donna, Lewis Fox's wife… she is where we need to start; however she has been institutionalized for eight years now in a psychiatric ward. She and Fox have a son; he's an attorney living in the Cayman Islands. No information indicates that the son is involved in any of the criminal enterprises of the Dixie Mafia. Their son appears to be pretty much estranged from his immediate family." Jones clicked the button on the remote one last time, yielding a solid black screen in front of them.

"Each of you has a complete file with all the information, photos, and reports we have available. We will have more intel from an informant within twenty four hours. When we can decipher the connection between these two organized crime families, we will be one step closer to taking out the hit man before he gets to our agent. Each of you is teamed up and has your assignments in the folder.

"Who are our points of contact in the Caymans?" Anthony asked.

You will be provided with the names of CIA and FBI Agents at that location. We will answer any questions and then take a quick break before resuming our meeting for some final details." Madison looked solemnly across the room before acknowledging Roberto who raised his hand.

"What you're proposing is sheer madness. You realize this, don't you? Operating off the grid, practically like outlaws, can't exactly be the most practical way to get the job done. There has to be a better way." Roberto argued.

Jones shook his head before replying. "Granted, you have a point, but this way, we don't have the bureaucracy or the constraints. Our CIA record is proof of it.

We use a small number of highly trained operatives and we don't shy away from extremely aggressive interventions.

We succeed by directing events the way we want them to proceed with a desirable outcome. You don't need vast overheads, just brains and guts."

"And blood," Grayson added.

Madison began giving out further directives. "Anthony will be going with a few team members to the Caymans to interview the attorney. Chase and Ashley will go to the psychiatric ward to question Donna. Brease and her team will work with the CIA operatives to discover the source of the leak."

"Ashley is not going anywhere near Fox or his wife! I didn't want her even being a part of this operation. Do you understand me?" Anthony announced sternly.

"Anthony, we understand your concern for your wife. In this operation, however, I am utilizing the best qualified operatives for the assignments at hand. Donna is a female, a daughter, a wife, a mother… She is more likely to open up to Ashley than anyone else. Need I say more?" Jones explained.

"I will go question her. I have more knowledge of their background than most, Anthony. Director Lawrence did send his last words to me before he killed himself." Ashley reminded him.

Jones cleared his throat loudly and looked at his watch. "Okay. Assignments have been made. There are just a few more details we need to iron out before leaving today. I want each of you to thumb to the back of the folders you were given. You will find a section containing a few photographs. I have some more coming.

These are members of both crime organizations; Colombian Drug Cartel and Dixie Mafia."

Jones was stunned, awestruck, and bewildered to the point of momentary speechlessness, when he saw the enormous shape suddenly looming outside the plate-glass window, abruptly appearing from out of nowhere.

He recognized it as a helicopter only at the instant that the rapid succession of bullets pierced numerous holes in the glass, the automatic machine-gun fire shattering the glass into a crystalline rainstorm.

Chase dove to the floor, pulling Ashley with him, both of them tumbling beneath the long conference table for cover. Pierce, the guy from ATF at the table to their right, closest to the window, had no such opportunity. He suffered a direct hit.

His hands flew out to his side like a bird about to take flight, and then his entire body thrashed grotesquely. Pierce let out a blood curdling scream as the bullets penetrated his face, skull, and chest.

Blood shot from his twitching body as his face contorted in a horrible full-throated scream. The deafening racket of the hovering helicopter muffled the sound of the ear-splitting gunfire. Wind rushed through the conference room, sending papers flying everywhere. From under the table, Chase saw Pierce splayed unnaturally on the carpet, the entire back of his head missing.

Ashley looked across the grey carpet, pitted by bullets, toward the front of the room and saw Anthony and Director Jones. Thank God, Anthony was okay.

"Clear the fucking room, NOW!" Jones screamed at everyone.

Anthony and Jones had ripped open the vault door and emerged with an FGM-148 Javelin anti-tank guided missile (ATGM) launcher.

"Get everyone the fuck out of here." Anthony tried yelling to Jones over the noise as he started pulling out the parts and assembling the launcher with rapid speed.

The weapons system consisted of two major parts: the disposable launch tube missile, and the reusable Command Launch Unit. Anthony had mated the CLU to a Javelin launch tube in record speed. Anthony hoped that it lived up to its reputation.

"Can you get a lock on the chopper?" Jones asked.

"We're about the find out." Anthony said, locating the helicopter and roughly centering it in the thermal sight, he then pressed the first trigger, which engaged thermal locking system. After the successful lock, the missile fired with the second trigger.

This missile had the ability to engage helicopters in the direct attack mode. The Javelin missile used a tandem warhead designed to defeat the reactive armor found on most modern choppers and tanks.

Anthony hoped like hell this thing would work.

The precursor charge explodes on contact, causing any reactive armor it hit to detonate and expend its energy, allowing the primary warhead to penetrate through and make direct contact with the base armor before detonating.

The missile was ejected from the launcher by a small charge so that it reached a safe distance from the team before the main rocket motors ignited Anthony was thankful it could be fired from within buildings without extensive preparations. Heart pounding, holding his breath, he fired. In a split second the missile was gone, he continued holding his breath.

"Target is locked in. Clear the damn room!" Anthony yelled. The missile streaked toward the retreating helicopter, swerving as it corrected its path, and headed right for the very heart of the black beast.

Chapter 8

Ashley raced from the conference room, away from the nightmarish scene of blood, machine-gun rounds, and broken glass. Once she reached the doorway, she looked back, hunting Anthony, unable to leave until she knew he was okay. She saw the helicopter lunge away from the building and circle back for another attack. An instant later she heard the explosion, which seemed to begin within the interior of the chopper and expand outward. Pieces of the black monster flew upward amid the dark smoke and thrusting flames. In some sort of odd sequence, there came another blast, even louder. And then another. And another.

The sky was filled with fire. Then, as suddenly as it had appeared, it had exploded into a
million pieces and was gone.

Most of the team assembled briefly in the hall. There were screams and shouts from the directors.

"Oh, Jesus Christ!"

"What the fuck happened?"

"How did they infiltrate this building?"

"Get out of here and in the hallway. Jones has been hit. Call the ambulance, quickly!" Anthony said, throwing his cell phone into Ashley's hand as he eased Jones down onto the hallway carpet.

"My God, Director Jones has been shot -- he's, oh God, he's bleeding everywhere, he's going to die," Brease said in a hollow voice.

"Chase, catch her!" Ashley yelled, just as Brease passed out. He moved quickly, barely getting a hold on Brease before she slid down to the floor, totally unconscious.

"Greg, get the smelling salts from your bag."

Chase said, cradling Brease's unresponsive body on his lap.

He tore the packet open with his teeth before gingerly waving it under her nose. Within seconds, her breathing became faster and faster until she regained consciousness.

"What happened?" she asked.

"You fainted," Chase told her.

"I have never fainted in my life."

"It happens sometimes," Ashley said soothingly.

"I guess as long as I have been with the CIA, I have pretty much pushed paper. You know, the witness protection programs. I haven't seen a lot of field action and never so much blood."

"Not everyone is cut out for field work. Greg, see if you can help Brease outside for some fresher air. Take one of the guards with you," Chase instructed.

"Wait. Is Director Jones going to be okay?" Brease asked in barely a whisper.

"He'll be fine. Go outside with Greg and see if the fresh air will help. You are going to have a massive headache," Ashley told her firmly.

Anthony looked down at Jones. "Hold on, buddy; we have help coming." Anthony applied pressure to the oozing gunshot wound above his heart, staring down into the face of his grey-haired mentor and boss. This was neither a random attack, nor a generalized attempt to kill whoever was present in the conference room. The gunfire had been aimed precisely at his boss. His wife, Ashley would have been the prime target, yet the helicopter had positioned its guns directly at Jones. Maybe they had been aiming for him when they saw him pull out the launcher.

They could have easily taken out the whole team, but most of the rounds hit the ceiling and floor.

Why go to all that effort, just to take out one man? He asked himself silently.

"Get everyone in the aircraft and out of here now. Go to the safe location. You go, too…" Jones' voice was so weak that it was a mere whisper.

"I will, but not until the medics get here to help you."

"Life flight will be here in six minutes," Ashley said looking down at Anthony's blood stained shirt and bleeding arm as she slipped his cell back in his pocket.

"Chase, assemble the team and get everyone on the aircraft immediately. Roberto and Grayson, take the guards with you and go to the vault in the basement. Pull all the canvas backpacks and duffle bags. They have everything we will need in them," Madison ordered.

"Come on, Ash." Chase gently tugged Ashley by the arm.

"No, I'm not leaving Anthony." She knelt down on her knees beside him and Director Jones.

"She's a stubborn little cuss. I see why you love her," Jones murmured.

"Ash, go to the plane. I'll be there shortly," Anthony commanded, leaning over and kissing her quickly on the lips.

"It's me they wanted. I baited them. You know, tried to flush them out. I just didn't think they could breach our security here. Didn't think they would retaliate this quickly. The leak goes deeper than I thought…." Jones said faintly, losing the strength to talk.

"Who were you trying to flush out?" Anthony asked, but Jones had fallen into unconsciousness, his chest barely rising and falling. He had lost too much blood.

Within seconds, the medics came running down the hallway, pulling two stretchers as Ashley stood to leave.

"I love you, Anthony," she called over her shoulder as she followed Chase and the team out to the runway.

"The other one is inside the conference room. Pierce, ATF guy, didn't survive. Transport him to our morgue at the CIA. Take Jones to Bay City Medical Center; they have a trauma unit on standby for him. These four guards will accompany you," Anthony informed the Chief Medic.

"Yes, sir," he answered as his staff began preparing Jones for transport.

Anthony walked down the hallway and slid his finger across the screen of his phone, activating the contact listing. He scrolled down, tapped the screen, and waited for an answer.

"Hey, my man Anthony. What's up?"

"Drake, we have a situation at the old airport outside of Bay City. I need you to get the best explosive experts you have on your team and get down here ASAP.

We were attacked. Director Jones took gunfire and went by life flight to the trauma center. We had one casualty, Pierce with ATF. I took out the chopper with an FGM-148 Javelin missile launcher."

"Damn. There won't be much left!" Drake whistled on the other end.

"I know. That's why I called you. If anyone can come up with any evidence, it will be you and your team. The debris trajectory will be north to northwest from the front of the building. It appeared to be some type of Black Hawk helicopter. The damn thing just flew right up to the conference room window and started spraying gunfire everywhere. The ammo pierced bulletproof glass!"

"I will get the team assembled and head that way within the hour. We won't have much daylight left by the time we arrive. Are you going to seal the area off?" Drake asked.

"Already done. There are ten guards posted along the perimeter with a couple of FBI, DEA and CIA agents located strategically on the inside of the building. We are going to safe house number one in the panhandle. Do you remember where that one is located?" Anthony asked.

"Been a few months, but I sure do. I will drop by tonight."

"That works. And can you contact Federal Aviation and get us a printout of everything that was airborne in this area this afternoon?"

"I can have that information sent securely to my laptop within forty-five minutes. I'll review it in flight and fill you in when I see you tonight."

"Thanks, Drake. I owe you big time."

"No problem, just have a cold one ready for me when I get there. I'll give you a call right before I land on the roof." Drake laughed as he ended the call.

Anthony took one last look around, picked up two briefcases, and headed down the empty corridor toward the runway. He noticed the gash on his upper right forearm bleeding heavily as he held the last exit door open for Roberto and Grayson's crew; they were heavily laden with backpacks and bulging duffle bags. The FGM-148 Javelin missile launcher was an awesome piece of precision weaponry. He had simply fired it too quickly, resulting in the kickback that sliced his upper arm.

Chase, Vince, and Greg met the team members on the stairs of the plane. Each one grabbed backpacks and duffle bags. Ashley met Anthony at the entrance.

"Oh, my God! You were shot!" She ushered him inside to the first aisle seat. Their earlier argument seemed insignificant now. She loved her arrogant, pig-headed husband.

"No, I haven't been shot. I shot the missile launcher before I had it fully positioned. The bitch kicked back and sliced my arm open." He grimaced, suddenly registering the pain. As bad as his arm hurt, it was nothing compared to the terror he felt knowing his Ashley could have been killed.

Ashley retreated to the cabin area of the plane and returned shortly with a large metal first aid box. Chase took a seat opposite Anthony.

"Strip out of the shirt, mister," Ashley demanded.

"Any other time, I would be delighted to strip for you, sweetheart. But wouldn't you rather wait until there's not an audience?" he teased, attempting to lighten the tension in the plane.

"Okay, asshole. Just bare your upper arm for me." Ashley started administering treatment to the wound on his arm.

"Sorry, babe for calling you a bitch earlier." Anthony looked over at Ashley.

"Yeah, yeah… I didn't mean to call you a fucking prick either." Ashley concentrated on treating the wound on his arm.

"I called Drake," he told Chase. "He's pulling his team together and headed this way to conduct an investigation on the debris from the chopper."

"Good deal. Did Jones say anything else?"

"Damn, Ash. That shit burns like hell. What did you pour on my arm?" Anthony snatched his arm away from Ashley.

She smiled innocently, pulling his arm back. "Just a little alcohol to cleanse the wound good, before I stitch it up."

"I think she's enjoying this too much!" Chase laughed loudly.

"Me, too," Anthony said with a grimace. "Jones lost consciousness after rambling about it being his fault for baiting them and trying to flush them out. He said he leaked information to them,
but I never got out of him who he was talking about."

"Apparently, he knew they would come after him, just not this soon. I think Jones has an idea who's behind the contract hit on Ash." Chase shook his head in disbelief.

"It just doesn't make any sense. That chopper could have killed all of us. For whatever reason, though, they retreated a safe distance. By the time I launched that missile, they were still circling but further away from the building."

"I'm sure if there is anything on the ground by way of evidence, John Drake and his team will find it quickly. What happened to him after he left DEA? I lost touch with him several years ago."

"He's the best I know. Drake freelances now for both the CIA and FBI. He was part of the team that went after Bin Laden and al Qaeda. With success might I add. Drake Industries in Ft. Lauderdale is owned by him.

They handle large scale private investigations, recon missions, governmental and personal protection. It is a very large company with a bunch of choppers, jets and planes. Where's Madison?" Anthony asked, looking around the plane.

"He has the other part of our team with him. He felt it was best if some of them drove to the safe house, instead of having the whole team on one flight. That way if something goes wrong… they don't kill all of us at one time." Chase tossed both hands upward by way of explanation.

"Probably,.. A good idea considering the way things have already gone down." Anthony said.

By the time Ashley had finished stitching Anthony's arm, the roar of the plane engines indicated they were in full flight ascending to slightly lower than normal altitude due to the short distance they would be traveling to the safe house.

She took the seat next to her husband and stared out the window of the plane. A faint red purplish tint was beginning to creep across the sky. The sun would be setting soon.

Funny, it seemed like a lot longer than just this morning, when she'd looked out this same window at the stars and moon glowing against a black velvet sky.

Anthony reached over, clasped her hand in his and gently squeezed, continuing his conversation with Chase. Ashley fumed and tried to tug her hand from his, but he gently tightened his grip. She was angry that he had kept her in the dark. She had a deep gut feeling that Anthony knew all along how high the price tag was on her head.

"I've never seen eyes like yours," he whispered as he leaned closer. "They're full of colors, like two kaleidoscopes when you're happy, and a dark raging sea when you're angry. Based on the way they look right now, I would say a major storm is brewing."

His voice rumbled through her, and his thumb stroked over her knuckles.

She was tipping toward him, helplessly caught up in his spell, the magic he wove when he wanted something.

"They don't really change from blue to green; it's just the lighting."

"I bet I could study your eyes for a long, long time," he said, "and never see all the color combinations."

Get control of yourself; he is only being nice because he wants you to go back to the island and stay under lock and key, Ashley mused silently to herself.

The next stretch of silence felt a little less comfortable, charged with something that she couldn't put into words. She had the oddest feeling that they'd both missed something... Something important. Something that could cost both of them an eternity. She shivered and quickly shrugged it off. There was no time for such thoughts.

Chapter 9

The plane began its descent, slowly dropping altitude. Ashley continued staring out the window below. Nothing was visible but the white caps of the ocean waves as they came down toward a seemingly abandoned stretch of beach. The plane veered sharply to the right, away from the coast and heading for tiny lights flickering in the distance. The closer they got, the larger and brighter the torches became, flooding light onto an abandoned long straight strip of sandy dirt road. The landing gears dropped and, suddenly, the plane was bumping down a narrow path with palm branches gently brushing the outer edges of the wings.

Just as the plane coasted to a stop, she noticed several rag top Jeeps, six big 4WD Chevy trucks lifted on their frames, and a couple of dark black SUV's.

"I hope this is our welcoming party?" Ashley raised a dark brow in question.

"Director Madison arranged for us to have transportation to the safe house via vehicles from this point. He wants us off this plane and out of here quickly," Chase answered.

"We needed the 4WD trucks to load all of our equipment. One of the SUV's has a full CIA extraction team inside. They will lead us to the safe house," Anthony explained.

"Let's get all our gear and get off this plane," Chase commanded his team.

"I'll take the black rag top Jeep." Ashley made claim to one of smallest vehicles in the convoy before them.

"I hope you remember how to drive a stick. You'd be better off riding with Chase. Unless you'll change your mind, stay on this plane, and go back to the island?" Anthony said.

"I should hope I remember how to drive a stick, since the first thing I ever drove was a John Deere tractor."

She flipped her long dark curls over her shoulder. "See you at the safe house, babe." And then she stood and marched down the center aisle of the plane and down the steps Roberto had just dropped. Ashley was in no mood for his patronizing attitude.

His moods were like a roller coaster, very quick heights only to drop down low just as rapidly. And sad part was... she responded the same way.

Anthony bit back a curse, considering the operation, and stalked off behind her thinking what a temperamental woman his wife had become.

She just would not listen to reason. He caught up with her as she was climbing into the Jeep and tossed a duffle bag into the backseat.

"Why must you be so difficult?" he asked under his breath.

"Me, difficult? Have you looked in the mirror lately, buddy?" She eased the strap of the backpack off her shoulder and tossed it in the Jeep as well.

"You should have stayed back where you would have been safe." He shook his head.

"No, you just don't want me working in law enforcement. You never have and never will...But it's fine. After this, we retire. It has cost both of us enough, don't you think?"

"Yes." Anthony gritted through his teeth, turned on his heel, almost colliding with Brease, and stormed off toward the dark SUV parked behind the Jeep.

Brease approached the Jeep. "Damn, is he okay? Mind if I ride with you?"

"Yeah, he's just being Anthony. And, of course you can. I would prefer your company to that of my overbearing asshole husband right now!"

"He has been acting a bit weird. What's up with him?" Brease asked.

"Anthony is arrogant, controlling, overprotective, and used to getting his way. We get along great, except when we try to work together. He just can't handle the thought of me getting hurt. He wasn't this bad, until I got shot in the last operation. Now he wants to lock me away so no one can every get to me… and buy me anything I want. It's hard to explain, I have always been very independent."

"Have you guys always argued this much?" Brease inquired.

Ashley gave a short laugh. "Pretty much. Sometimes I don't know why I love his stupid ass. But, he really is my knight in shining armor. His armor just has a lot of dents in it"

Brease gave her an understanding smile as she tossed two duffle bags into the back seat before sliding into the passenger seat.

"It's going to be a hot one tonight."

"I agree," Ashley said, already wiping the perspiration from her face. The fear crawling around in her chest made her lips tighten. Damn it. This was precisely why she'd originally wanted them to retire after they married. She had lost Anthony once and now the possibility that either or both of them could die during this operating scared her to death.

Their son could lose both his parents. Reflecting back, Ashley went into law enforcement when she was twenty.

She was idealistic and was going to save the world. It didn't take long to realize how corrupt the justice system could be in some areas. You spent more time doing paperwork than some of the assholes you arrested actually spent in jail. This job was tough on any marriage. She knew that Gina and Larry and Brenda and Chase had suffered the same problems due to being married to a cop. She and Anthony had a double obstacle to overcome; they were both cops.

Forcing aside her thoughts, she put the Jeep in gear and watched as Anthony got into the back of the big black

SUV.

Ashley eased in behind them, glancing in her rearview mirror to see Chase pulling in behind her. She always rode with her window slightly open so she could hear the outside noises.

The crisp clean salty air assaulted her senses, bringing back a flood of memories.

The almost full moon illuminated the sandy dirt trail as the team made their way up its winding path. An overgrowth of moss dangling from the oak trees created eerie shadows at each bend in the road.

"How long do you think this operation will last?" Brease broke the silence.

"It's hard to say. I've stayed undercover for nine, ten months before. Working together as a team instead of solo, it usually culminates quicker. We could finish up in as little as four or five days."

"I hope it's the latter. I miss Patrick," Brease admitted.

"I know. It seems like just when we were all getting to the good stuff in our lives, all hell broke loose." Ashley shook her head.

"You know Patrick wants me to take a desk job?

He doesn't want me doing anything in law enforcement."

"What do you want to do?" Ashley took her eyes off the road briefly and glanced over at Brease.

"I honestly don't know. I mean I pretty much have a desk job with the CIA. I have never thought of doing anything else…"

"Well, this is certainly not a field of work that's good for a marriage," Ashley said regretfully.

"How do you and Anthony survive the work?"

She gave a derisive laugh. "Sometimes we don't. We're not getting along very well right now because I refused to stay home under lock and key."

"I sensed the tension between you guys," Brease said sympathetically.

"It is a little more than tension. We have always locked horns so to speak with regards to work. He becomes a dictator and I rebel…"

"I'm seeing a little of that in Patrick right now and I don't know why. I mean, we met because of my work with the CIA. I arranged his protective custody in the last operation. Do you think you could talk to him for me?" she asked Ashley.

"Sure, I'll try. I know he really loves you and worries about your safety. You have to decide what you want to do first, though. You can't give up a part of yourself to make someone else happy. It just doesn't work."

"Do you feel like that's what you've done? Given up a part of yourself?"

"Sometimes. Don't get me wrong I love Anthony with all my heart. We went through some really rough years before he left and then he just showed back up. We didn't take the time to heal from old hurts; we were married within a matter of months of him being released from the hospital.

Both of us went back to the work that destroyed us before.

He and I made each other a promise this time. We have hit a crossroads in life and there will be no more undercover or special operations in our future."

"Do you think you've both become jaded?" Brease asked.

"I am sure we have, but justice is more jaded than either of us. I wish there were such a thing as Eternal Justice!"

"How do you handle having a price on your head?"

Ashley didn't have an answer and simply shook her head. "I don't know, it's not the first one, it's just the highest dollar one."

Twenty minutes later, engrossed in her own thoughts, she nearly rear-ended the SUV in front of her when it took a sharp right turn onto another narrow sandy drive.

"Damn!" Ashley shouted, throwing her hands upward.

"You could have given me some warning that you were going to turn, asshole!" She had downshifted and braked so quickly that the Jeep had stalled, causing Chase to nearly smash her in back. Ashley cranked the Jeep and shifted gears quickly in an effort to catch up with the diminishing tail-lights of the SUV. She glanced over to see Brease holding on for dear life.

A pair of enormous wrought iron gates greeted them at the end of the drive. Anthony got out and punched a code on the keypad and the gates parted. The team pulled through the gates and arrived at the well-manicured, beautifully landscaped grounds of the safe house. The air was hot and humid and smelled of gardenias and a freshly mown lawn.

The massive peach colored stucco structure was two stories high with a porch running across the front and down both sides.

All the windows had bars, as did the front entrance door. The perimeter was marked by a ten foot high iron fence. Motion lights on the front of the house had activated when the first vehicle came within thirty feet, flooding the whole area with bright light.

Two armed guards stood on either side of the front entrance. Ashley looked behind them and saw the iron gates slowly closing as the last vehicle entered. This is like being in prison or a horror movie, she thought to herself.

She and Brease got out of the Jeep. From the corner of her eye, she noticed Anthony had squared his shoulders, a sure sign he was pissed off about something. His wide mouth was creased in a frown as she stepped closer to him.

His dark-eyed gaze rested on her briefly before shifting to the body builder looking guy who exited the vehicle with him.

Given the way he studied the other man, there might as well have been a sign tattooed on his forehead with the words testosterone overload.

She stifled a sigh. "What's wrong ,Anthony?"

He ran his hand through his jet black hair before lowering it to clasp her by the wrist. He led her away from the team. "I told you not to come, to stay the hell at home."

"What are you so pissed about now?" Ashley bristled at his words.

"Mr. Don Juan CIA dude over there!" He gestured toward the guy walking toward the massive house behind them.

"What about him?"

"When I got in the SUV with them as we were leaving the drop site, he was telling the other two guys how fucking hot the tall dark-haired bitch
looked and how he would 'do that' before this
operation was over." Each word dripped with
sarcasm.

"Oh, my God. Anthony, we are not in high school. Ignore the bastard; we have more important things to worry about."

"I'll ignore him all right. Right after I beat his face in the dirt."

"This is ridiculous..." She opened her mouth to say more, but his hand suddenly dug into her waist.

"I don't like it... I told him that was my fucking wife he was talking about!" His jaw twitched.

"I am sure he won't say or do anything else. Besides, I can take care of myself. We are a team, remember?"

Anthony swallowed back his anger. "All right." His tone was composed and friendlier, but the hard set of his broad shoulders revealed that he still wasn't pleased with the turn of events.

"I love you," Ashley said.

A spark of humor lit his dark eyes. "Have you forgotten what I do for a living, sweetheart? I'm a mercenary now. We live and breathe covert. Don't worry. If he so much as looks at you the wrong way...."

Ashley's anger thawed a little, replaced by a warm rush that surrounded her heart. Licking her dry lips, she tilted her head to meet his eyes. "Just maintain your composure, babe."

"I will. I'm sorry, you're the best thing that ever happened to me and I'll make sure you're safe." Anthony ran his hand through his hair again, frustrated with himself for losing control. He really had to get a grip. Ashley was right; this job was literally killing them both.

She walked past the two guards, opened the door, and motioned for Anthony to follow her into the front foyer. White marble spanned the enormous space. She flicked the switch and the foyer lit up via a huge chandelier, revealing two spiral staircases leading to the second floor; one on the east side and one on the west side.

"Oh my God." She shivered as she stared up at the massive chandelier.

"It reminds you of the one that came crashing down at the Martinelli Mansion, doesn't it? Anthony asked.

"Yes, it does," she said.

They walked around the barrier wall to an enormous kitchen that boasted so much glossy black marble and stainless steel it made their eyes hurt. He didn't remember this safe house being so opulent. The rest of the team began canvassing the entire house with stunned expressions.

"They renovated this place for someone of great importance?" Chase asked.

"My sentiments exactly. It's been a while since I've

been here, but it certainly didn't look like this," Anthony agreed.

"Everybody pick a bedroom upstairs and meet back down in the conference room in thirty," Chase hollered down the foyer.

Ashley and Anthony found the last bedroom on the far corner of the west wing. She opened the door and glanced around the huge room. Dropping her gear and luggage, she wandered into the bathroom suite. A massive whirlpool tub beckoned from the corner. The linen closet was packed full of fresh towels, linens, and any kind of toiletry product one could imagine.

"Look at the size of this bathroom! It is larger than our whole bedroom," she exclaimed.

"Sure is," Anthony said, peering around the corner.

She walked back into the bedroom, stopping beside Anthony, who was inches from the bed. Her legs bumped against the corner. She was just inches from him.

"Ashley, how do you put up with me? You know, I promise…"

"Anthony, don't say it unless……"

"Unless I mean it? But I do." His left hand lifted and pressed lightly against the line of her jaw. "Ashley, I love you and this will be our final operation. I have something for you." He reached down and unzipped his canvas duffle bag, retrieving a square box with tiny green ribbons curled around the top.

"You shouldn't have," she said softly as she untied the ribbons surrounding the light green crown-embossed box. She lifted the lid off to reveal a dark green leather jewelry box inside. Cocking her head, puzzled, she removed the leather box and popped open the lid. Inside was the most exquisite Rolex Pearlmaster she had ever seen. The Tahitian mother of pearl face with roman markers was covered by sapphire crystals.

"Do you like it?" he asked as he lifted the watch out of the box, opened the hidden clasp, and held it down for her to read.

"Always with You. Love, T," Ashley read the tiny script engraving.

"Oh, Anthony, I love it. It says it's waterproof. I will never take it off!"

"Well, let's put it on you and take everything else off?"

He kissed her and his mouth took hers, rough, hungry, because he couldn't hold back. He needed her too much. Always had. The pain of the past years --- of being without her---- didn't matter anymore. The past was the past and they were given a second chance. She was his wife; she was with him now. In his arms, and he was going to make up for all the times he had hurt her in the past.

He pulled her even closer. She stumbled against the bed and laughed against his mouth. That laugh was the sweetest sound he'd ever heard. He was going to spend the rest of his life making her happy, hearing her laugh and seeing the light in her sapphire blue eyes. His tongue slid past her lips and tasted that laughter. So sweet. Just like her.

"Anthony…" she whispered, as she pulled her lips from his. "We can't. We have to meet downstairs in thirty….."

"I am locking the door." Hell, this wasn't the time. Not the place. "I'm a greedy bastard," he confessed as he clicked the lock on their door.

An answering smile, slow and sexy, curved her lips. She kissed him, her head dipped toward him. Her mouth, wet, hot, and open, found his. She kissed him with a passion that had his body tensing and wondering just how much privacy they'd be able to get.

Later, there was banging on the door. "Come on, you guys. You're holding the meeting up.

We have a lot of ground to cover. Director Madison sent me after you. He's ready and wants to start the meeting early." Chase said.

Anthony glanced at the door, slapping Ashley on the butt as he rolled off the bed. "We'll be down in ten," he called as he headed for the shower. "Come on," he said to Ashley. "This has to be a two for one. You wash my back and I'll wash......" He smiled provocatively.

Her grin flashed. "You're such an ass! But you're my ass."

Chapter 10

Everyone was seated in the conference room by the time she and Anthony arrived for the meeting. They arrived on time, but she felt every eye in the room turn and stare at them as they walked in to take a seat as Madison wanted to start the meeting early.

"Just show up when you feel like it," Chase said with a laugh.

"Oh, shut up!" Ashley said.

"You guys could have waited until later," he whispered in her ear.

"You're just jealous because Brenda isn't here and you can't get any," she hissed back.

"Probably." He grinned.

"You two must have learned to whisper in a saw mill," Anthony said.

A muffled giggle came from Brease, seated on the other side of Chase.

"I'll admit it... I'm jealous as hell." Brease said quietly.

****

"Let me have everyone's attention, please. We've all had a long day already but we still have much to cover. You have laptops in front of you. We'll go through all the information first and answer questions at the end. Greg, the Information Technician with DEA, will proceed with the presentation," Director Madison informed the team.

"Let's have it, geek boy!" Chase laughed.

"Chase, that's rude. Don't call him that," Ashley said.

"It's okay; I know Chase really has the hots for me," Greg replied.

"Okay, let's get serious here now. This is a matter of life and death. I know from being a cop for twenty five years that humor is the only way we know how to deal with stressful situations. I remember my second year on the force attending an autopsy and watching the medical examiner eat a sandwich while performing an autopsy. We do what we have to in order to camouflage how we really feel about the atrocities we see and experience. All the same, let's get grounded and plan this thing out in detail." Madison commanded the team.

The laughter quickly settled down, Greg proceeded with the entire layout of the operation. We will have most of the same team members we had for the last operation.

We will utilize a team staying behind here to follow leads and continue interrogation of informants.

It is essential that we get to the son of Lewis Fox. He may be able to shed some light on his father's current business activities and the whereabouts of the Dixie Mafia. It is troublesome that the package that was received, the monogramed handkerchief to be exact, is a calling card used by Lewis Fox. That is the only thing we have linking this hit to the DM. The DNA is that of a dead man, the son of the Colombian Drug Cartel Leader, who is also dead. We are sending Anthony and Drake to located Samuel Fox, Lewis S. Fox son. The plan is for initial contact to be made for identification purposes as Samuel has remained anonymous for years. No photos exist for comparison; he has no fingerprints on file or in any database as he has no arrest record.

Once positive ID is established, then he will be interviewed, followed by interrogation if necessary. Another team will be sent to interview Lewis Fox wife, Donna. The floor was opened for questions as every team member studied his or her assigned role for the operation.

"Do we know yet, what the connection is between the Mafia and the Cartel?" Anthony asked.

"No, that is a key element of the operation. If we can determine this connection, we will be one step closer to determining who contracted the hit." Greg responded.

"I have already mentioned to Drake that I will need him to partner up with me on this one. His company can provide the aircraft to get any of us to designated locations quickly without a lot of attention being drawn."

"That is going to be an essential part of Operation Crossroads. Everything we do must be covert. We can't afford to bring attention to any one of us.

With this kind of money on the table, there will be a lot of takers to perform a professional hit." Greg clicked the remote he held in his hand, bringing the most recent photographs up on the plasma screens. Slide after slide of Mafia and Cartel henchmen and troops filled the screens.

"Are these photographs recent?" Anthony questioned.

"Yes, and everyone needs to study each one in detail. There is a short bio beneath each picture. This gives you the information we have at our disposal. As you can see, you have a variety of expert marksmen and demolition experts." Greg used the pointer to indicate these on the screen.

"Have we taken into consideration the fact that if this is a personal vendetta contract hit, the contractor may want to actually perform the deed himself?" Anthony asked.

"Yes, that is why we are targeting Samuel and Donna. They are the closest immediate
relatives to Lewis Fox. They may have beneficial information and not even realize the importance of what they know." Greg continued.

"How are we so sure that there is a connection between the Dixie Mafia and the Colombian Drug Cartel?" Ashley asked.

"The last major arms traffickers we arrested yesterday were a combination of both groups. DEA also arrested major traffickers last week and the group consisted of members from both organized crime families." Greg replied.

"Who is running the Colombia Drug Cartel since Adrianno Martinellis and his son Ricky are dead?" Chase asked.

"We don't know right now. We have a very good confidential informant that is inside the Cartel. He is meeting with one of our agents as we speak to update us on current activities involving the group.

Let's go back through the photographs of known organized crime leaders and members of each group. You each have folders containing this information. We will take them one by one, if any of you have had dealings with one of them, we need the information." Greg proceeded to add notes to each screen using his laptop.

"The one on the right, I arrested ten years ago for heroin trafficking. He was with the Colombians then, not the Mafia." Chase said.

"Okay. So there is even more evidence of the merger between these two crime families." Greg added this information.

"Go back to the slide of Ricky Martinelli's funeral." Ashley said.

Greg clicked the remote several times. "This one?"

"Yes. I just wanted to see if we could recognize anyone odd at the funeral services." Ashley said.

"I don't see anyone suspect." Chase said staring up at the plasma TV.

"Look at the man on the far right in the very back. That is Forcont, the owner of the Mustang Ranch in Nevada. He was charged with the murder of that boxer that had an affair with Donna, Fox's wife. It was a brutal murder, shot six times and stabbed twenty-six times. There was a monogramed handkerchief like the one I received, shoved down his throat. He fled to Brazil where he couldn't be extradited and has never been arrested. He is on the most wanted list." Ashley said pointing at the picture.

"You're right. He and Adrianno Martinelli were business partners." Anthony stated.

"So, maybe it isn't Fox that is behind the hit on Ashley. Maybe it is Forcont?" Roberto added.

"This doesn't make any sense. Why would the Colombian Drug Cartel be in business with the
man Fox contracted to kill his wife's lover?" Chase asked.

"I still think it is Fox. I just don't know why or how, Martinelli and Fox are connected." Ashley replied.

"It's possible that FBI Director was wrong. If you look back at the suicide note he left, he implied that Fox contracted Forcont to kill the boxer. Maybe Forcont did it alone?" Greg clicked back to the copy of the suicide note.

"I don't think so; Lawrence killed himself because he was on the Dixie Mafia payroll and realized Victor Shayne was actually Anthony, undercover CIA." Ashley shook her head.

"There is definitely a lot of information tying the two organized crime families together. Which is surprising, considering how many cases all of us worked in the past where the two murdered each other's members." Chase said.

"Fox really doesn't have a reason to go after Ashley. If it were Fox, he would be more likely to put out a hit on Anthony." Grayson added.

"Unless… the hit on Ashley was initiated by Fox to destroy me." Anthony said through gritted teeth.

Two hours later, dinner was served in the dining room. The safe house had a chef in residence at all times.

They had Blue Crab Cake appetizers served with roasted red peppers, and Bourguignon Beef stewed in a red wine sauce with carrots and pearl onions. Crème Brulee followed, with its creamy custard and sugar top caramelized to perfection. They devoured their food and were discussing final details when their chef returned to refill their drinks. Ashley read the name on the pristine white jacket.

"Thank you, Pierre."

"My pleasure, madame," he answered in a distinct French accent before quickly exiting the room.

"He defected from France. Pierre was the Marsella Family chef for twenty years. His information brought down the whole French connection trafficking in drugs, prostitution, murder and illegal gambling," Anthony whispered in Ashley's ear.

"The Marsella Mafia? I worked a drug case involving them about ten years ago." she asked in disbelief.

"Yes. The safe house has been his home for almost ten years now. The case you worked would have been a result of the information Pierre provided. Pierre left everything behind in France, bringing only his impeccable culinary skills with him. I met him years ago, but I never knew where he was placed once he entered witness protection," Anthony said with a half-smile as he glanced down at his cell to read an incoming text.

"What the hell is that?" Ashley jumped from her seat, as a loud whipping sound from overhead vibrated the walls. She and Chase stared at each other, .45 and 9mm drawn. Every team member had immediately assumed a defensive posture.

"Everyone calm down. Holster your weapons. I just received a text from Drake. He's landing his chopper on the roof," Anthony said.

Chase slid his 9mm SIG across his palm. In three efficient moves, he had the ammo checked, the safety back on, and the gun covered with his shirt.

"Shit! You could have warned us," Ashley said, holstering her firearm.

"Yeah, man. That's a good way to get your ass shot," Roberto chimed in.

"My apologies." Anthony smiled, opening the hallway door which led to the roof.

"Hey, it smells fantastic in here. You guys didn't save dinner for me?" Drake called as he entered the hallway outside the dining room.

"Most of you know him, but for those of you who don't, this is Drake."

"Hey, Drake, it's been a long time," Chase said, shaking his hand.

"Monsieur Drake, I will bring you appetizers and make you a dinner plate." Pierre hurried off to the kitchen just as quickly as he had entered.

"Grand entrance, Drake! You almost got your ass shot," Ashley said as they headed back to the dining table.

"Little Flamingo, you wouldn't shoot me, now would you?" he asked.

"Why have you always called me that? I'm 5'10" and you're only four inches taller than I am. I'm not little."

"But, you don't have these smooth, sculpted pecs and ab or a full six pack." He pulled up his snug fitting AC/DC tank shirt to prove just that by flexing his muscles.

"You were always younger, faster, and flashier than us and you used to have those stupid flamingo chimes that you moved with you every time you relocated."

"Well, this little flamingo is the source of a huge problem. Did you get all the intel I emailed you?" Anthony asked.

"Yep, I reviewed it.... wait until I fill you guys in on what we found at the scene. Who the hell did you piss off?" Drake asked, shaking his head.

"We think it's the Colombians or it could be the Dixie Mafia," Anthony answered.

"I can't think of any nicer guys to piss off." Drake said laughing.

"Curiosity is killing me. What did you find?" Chase asked.

"My guys combed the entire area. I had a couple of jets and a chopper fly in to take custody of the evidence for testing. Ever heard of a MH-60 Black Hawk stealth helicopter?" he asked, his British accent slightly detectable.

"You're shitting me? They didn't make but two of those, did they?"

"Right. One of two specially modified MH-60's, which were used in the raid on Osama bin Laden's hideout in Pakistan. It was damaged in the hard landing and destroyed by U.S. forces. That one was modified with reduced noise signature and stealth technology. It has special coatings and anti-radar treatments for the windshields. This was that MH-60 stealth with some adaptations for firing systems, rockets, and machine guns."

"Are you sure?" Anthony asked.

"Absolutely. I know where the only other one is located. The modifications your attacker made added several hundred pounds, making it susceptible to crashing. The same thing happened in Pakistan. The pieces of the gearbox, rotor blades, refueling probe, and cockpit that we recovered are an exact match to the one Special

Forces downed. I have no damn idea how it was reassembled and brought back to life, but it's the same one."

Anthony let out a soft whistle. "So the bad guys managed to steal a classified piece of military weaponry. Not just any weaponry, but one that was destroyed a couple of years ago. I think the leak is going to be a lot higher up than we originally thought."

"How does this new information affect the operation?" Ashley met Anthony's gaze with a frown.

"We can't trust anyone outside our immediate team. You need to leave this operation now, Go home where we can place guards twenty-four seven." he demanded.

"Unbelievable," she huffed as she stared up at him. "This is exactly what I expected out of you. The package with the scarf in it was addressed to me, not to mention the

DNA is that of a dead guy, one I killed. The contract hit is out on my head. I am a cop. I will not tuck my tail, run, and hide." She scowled.

"Dammit, man. Your wife still has a hot little temper. But she has a point. If you were in her shoes, you would be the same way." Drake went on. "You know, I think it might be more fruitful if we focused on finding out who sent that package. Besides, she will be safe here with the team."

"I agree. They obviously wanted Ash to know they were coming for her. Director Jones kept saying there was a connection between the Columbian Cartel and the Dixie Mafia. The suicide note that FBI Director Lawrence left did tie the two together via money laundering, but I think it goes deeper. Lawrence's daughter, the one married to Fox, is still in a psychiatric ward. She has been
for years. I think we need to start by seeing if she is
coherent." Chase let out a breath.

"I think talking to Donna is a good idea." Ashley added.

"You're going to be the death of me." Anthony stared at her in exasperation.

"Okay, my guys will work the evidence on the Black Hawk. We can track it back to find out who fronted that kind of money. Who is the hot little blonde at the end of the table, by the way?" Drake asked with a smile.

"My cousin's fiancé, Brease. She works for the CIA," Ashley informed him.

"Now that everyone has regrouped, I say we revert to our original plan. We have a little more information now." Anthony said.

"Okay. Anthony, you and I will take Brease on a little trip to the Caymans? She is a good looking little thing. Should be enough to turn the head of a rich lawyer, don't you think?" Drake asked.

"Probably. We can let Madison know about the operational change, that we're taking Brease. We have very little information on this guy. No photos, nothing. Just his name, Lewis Samuel Fox, II.

Fox Sr. did a good job keeping him hidden all these years," Anthony said.

"Chase and I will go to the East Coast. We can talk to Director Lawrence's daughter, Donna," Ashley said.

"I'll have my company jets fly into the nearest airport. We can take the chopper and fly out from there early in the morning," Drake offered.

"Works for me. Roberto and Grayson will be in charge here. There are a lot of leads they can follow up on locally," Chase said.

"Let's get everyone back to the conference room and iron out all the details. Most of it will go as already planned. We will fly out in the morning."

Ashley wordlessly watched Anthony walk away. When he disappeared from view, she walked back over to the dining room table. She'd left one of the files on the table. She made her way across the foyer to the conference room. Her back and neck muscles ached as she sank into the leather chair, making her realize she had a migraine coming on. With a sigh, she flipped the laptop open and began reviewing the intel for the operation again. About twenty minutes later, her cell phone vibrated. She removed it from the clip at her waist and recognized Aunt Lynn's number.

"Hello?"

"Sweetie, A.J. wanted to call and say hi. Is this a bad time?" Aunt Lynn asked.

"It's okay. I can take a quick break. I'm sure Chase told you how bad the day has been. Put A.J. on." Ashley walked out into the foyer to talk to her son.

"Hey, Momma. What are you and Daddy doing?" A.J. asked.

"Working, honey. Are you having fun with Aunt Lynn, Brenda, and Craig?"

"Oh, yeah. Craig climbed a palm tree to get Leo's Frisbee back from that damn monkey."

"Anthony John, you don't curse. Who have you heard saying that word?" Ashley asked.

"Craig. He says damn all the time, I mean that word." A.J. continued to chatter excitedly about swimming with Brenda and scalloping with Craig while Aunt Lynn grilled burgers.

"Can I talk to daddy?"

"No, sweetie, not right now. Daddy is busy, he will call you in the morning, okay?

"Okay. I miss you," he said with a sniffle.

"We miss you, too. Be good. I love you. Let me talk to Aunt Lynn or Brenda for a minute, okay?"

A.J. smacked kisses to the phone before handing the phone off to Brenda.

"Hi. Your aunt just took Leo out for a walk. Vince is with her."

"Is everything okay there?" Ashley asked.

"We're fine. Vince doesn't let us out of his site. Craig is keeping A.J. busy. How are you holding up?"

"Good. Chase and I are going to follow up on some leads in the morning. Hopefully, we can finish this operation quickly."

"Okay, honey. I love you. Tell Chase I'll call him later."

Brenda hung up. Ashley's fingers tightened over the phone briefly before sliding it back in the case. She sighed as she walked back into the conference room. Anthony was engrossed in conversation with Greg. They were obviously ironing out some of the computer or technical issues that would be involved.

"We just received an update on Jones," Chase said. "He came out of the second surgery okay and is holding his own in recovery. Hopefully, by tomorrow afternoon, he can tell us something. They will be keeping him sedated through the night and morning hours."

"That's good news." She glanced down at her new watch. "It's already ten thirty"

He yawned. "Yeah. I am washed out."

"Me, too. I hope they're wrapping everything up since we're leaving early in the morning. It's hard to believe it's just Wednesday night. Four nights ago, we were all happy and celebrating Anthony's birthday." She frowned.

"I know. I caught a few winks on the plane but not enough." He yawned again.

"Stop, that's contagious," Ashley said, stifling a yawn.

"Okay, everyone, it's very late," Madison addressed the team, "and we have an early morning tomorrow. You have your assignments. We will plan on meeting back here on Friday morning for updates. The team staying behind will

be led by Roberto and Grayson and will keep each other informed as they go along. I'll be at the hospital tomorrow, waiting until Jones is out of recovery so I can talk to him as soon as he is able to speak."

Ashley tossed the files in her briefcase and clicked it shut before heading out of conference room toward the staircase. Anthony stood patiently waiting at the foot of the stairs with his hand extended.

"May I escort Mrs. Langston to her suite?" he asked seductively.

"Why of course," she replied in an exaggerated Southern voice.

Chapter 11

East Coast of Florida
Thursday Morning
11:45 a.m.

After two hours of driving, they were about forty-five minutes from the little town of New Haven on the south central coast of Florida. The private jet had gotten them to the Jacksonville airport in record time and a rental SUV had been waiting. The New Haven Long Term Psychiatric Hospital had an ocean front view.

Ashley and Chase had acquired credentials as a psychiatrist and psychologist conducting field research for grants on long-term psychiatric care patients. They would have one shot to get Donna to talk. It was doubtful, though, based on her medical file. She was on Thorazine, an older anti-psychotic with long term side effects of permanent brain damage.

Ashley looked down at the photograph of Donna. She was a gorgeous, classy-looking blonde. Big blue eyes graced her heart shaped, porcelain looking face. The picture was about ten years old.

"Chase, isn't that our exit coming up?" Ashley pointed.

"Yep, that takes us down to the coast. Hospital should be about four miles ahead on the left, at the last major crossroads."

She popped the lid on her briefcase and pulled out a pair of dark horn-rimmed glasses.

"Well, how do I look?" she asked after slipping the non-prescription glasses low on the bridge of her nose.

"Like a nerdy professor, especially with your hair up in a bun." He laughed.

"Thanks, that's the look I'm trying to achieve," she replied with a sarcastic smile.

"Well, you're spot on honey! Blazer, slacks and… well the cowboy boots do look a little odd." He couldn't stop laughing.

"I hope you don't act like this in the ward. They will think we need to live here!" Ashley said in joking reprimand.

"Hey, Nerdy Professor.... I got this. You just worry about getting information out of Donna," he said.

As he parked the dark SUV, across the garage a snazzy red Porsche peeled out onto the highway at a high rate of speed. Some people just don't know how to drive. That kind of behavior gets people killed, Ashley thought. They exited the vehicle and locked the doors. She and Chase looked at each other, shook their heads, and headed for the main entrance of the hospital. As they approached the sliding glass doors, Chase pressed the intercom and waited.

"Welcome to New Haven Long Term Facility. How can we help you?" a clinical sounding female attendant asked through the speaker.

"I am Dr. Evans, accompanied by Dr. Slidel. We have an appointment to tour the facility and interview patients."

"One moment please. Okay, please make sure you have no weapons and enter through the doors to your right," the attendant instructed. The buzzer went off and the doors slid open. Ashley and Chase walked through, immediately greeted by facility security.

"Walk through the metal detector one at a time," The guard instructed. After their I.D. badges were checked, they were allowed through and told to have a seat in the lobby, where someone would be with them shortly.

A dark-haired, middle-aged man in a navy blue pin-striped suit met them at the lobby entrance nearly an hour later.

"Good morning, Dr. Evans and Dr. Slidel. I apologize for the delay. We are pleased to have you here and look forward to the possibility of additional funding sources for the facility. I am Mr. Noland, the administrator. My assistant, Andrea, will take you back to the counseling rooms where you will set up to conduct your patient interviews."

They followed Andrea, a petite, dark-haired woman, down the corridor. To the right of the swinging doors appeared to be a dayroom filled with patients. Two men and a woman appeared to be having a strained discussion. A security guard was headed that way. The lady stormed outside of the room and one of the men followed; the other filtered back into the room of patients.

Maybe not such a good sign. Ashley lingered at the door, watching the couple. The woman slapped the man; he crushed her against the wall.

"Well, hell." Ashley mumbled.

The security guard strode toward the two patients, just in time to grab the man's arm before he slapped the blonde. He whipped the guy around and shoved him back.

"Time for you to go into lockdown." Behind him the woman took off.

"That bitch started it," the guy yelled.

"Whatever the problem," the security guard warned, "you don't hit another patient. You walk away."

Ashley continued to peer through the glass window. A frown tugged at her brow when the blonde started ranting. *What the hell is she doing now?* She stood by the edge of the desk and was tearing up pieces of newspaper and eating it. The woman looked vaguely familiar.

Chase hesitated in the hallway and cleared his throat. "Dr. Slidel, we need to get started with the interviews. Andrea is going to take me on a tour of the facility while you start interviewing patients. She has given us a list. Just pick the one or ones you want to interview and she will bring them in for you."

Ashley glanced over the list and followed Chase and Andrea into the large office where she would be conducting the interviews. "I would like to start with Donna Fox," she said.

"Are you sure?" Andrea asked.

"Yes," Ashley replied.

"Okay, Dr. Slidel. I will get her for you." Andrea closed the door.

"I wonder why she asked if you were sure about interviewing Donna?" Chase asked.

"I don't have a clue."

"Okay. When she returns with Donna, make the time count." Chase pointed to his watch.

"I got this." Ashley smiled and tapped the Rolex on her wrist which Anthony had given her as a gift just last night.

Moments later, Andrea returned with Donna. Ashley stood for a second, only mildly surprised. Donna was the blonde who had slapped the man in the dayroom and then ate newspaper.

"Donna, sit down right here in front of this desk. This is Dr. Slidel. She is going to talk to you for a little while. You have to be on your best behavior. I will be just outside the door in my office." Andrea smiled reassuringly as she exited the room.

"Donna, I am Dr. Slidel. Is it okay if we talk?" Ashley asked.

"I guess," Donna answered, twirling her hair around her finger like a little girl.

"How long have you been here?" Ashley asked, trying to gauge Donna's grasp of time and reality.

"Too damn long," she snapped.

"Do you have many visitors? Does your family come and visit?" Ashley asked softly.

"Sometimes my son comes to see me. Lewis, my husband, never comes." Donna frowned.

"What is your son's name?"

"Samuel. That is really his middle name. His full name is Lewis Samuel Fox II. We always called him Sammy. He was named after his daddy." Donna nervously twisted her hair around her finger.

"Samuel is a nice name. Do you remember when he last came to visit?"

"It's been too long. I don't know." Donna's eyes filled with tears.

Ashley quickly thumbed through the medical chart to the visitation log. "You've been here a little over seven years. It looks like your son hasn't visited in over a year?"

"He's dead. My son is dead." Donna began to cry and pull at her hair.

"Your son is not dead. I'm sure he has been really busy working and hasn't been able to come and visit," Ashley said, trying to console Donna.

"No, he's dead. My daddy is dead. I miss my daddy. I want my daddy." Donna curled up in a fetal position on the floor and rocked back and forth.

Ashley knelt down on the floor beside Donna. "Look at me; your son is not dead. I will find him and get him to come and see you. I bet he's handsome. What does he look like?"

"He is tall like his daddy and has my daddy's eyes," she said with a sniffle.

"What type work does he do?" Ashley asked.

"My daddy was FBI."

"Okay. What type work does your son do?"

"He's a lawyer. My momma is dead, too." Donna looked up, her big blue eyes filled with tears.

"Do you know where your son lives?"

"He is in Heaven with my daddy and my momma." Donna began to sob hysterically and rock back and forth again.

"It's going to be okay, Donna." Ashley said quietly. There was no way of knowing the trauma inflicted on this young woman by her husband Lewis Fox.

Moments later Ashley got up off the floor and walked to the desk, pushing the intercom button. "You can come and get Donna now."

Within minutes, Andrea came through the door with an orderly. They gave Donna an injection, lifted her from the floor, and ushered her from the room. Ashley took out her phone out and began flipping through the chart and snapping pictures, page after page. There was a lot of information in the file that had not previously been provided to them. Donna's mother had never been to visit; the counseling and therapy notes indicated that her mother blamed her for her father's suicide.

The one thing that jumped out at her was the date of Donna's last visitor, over a year ago. It was seven days after Director Lawrence's suicide, four days after Ashley had shot and killed Ricky Martinelli and Fox had escaped. She wondered how the name of the visitor was omitted. That was illegal but when did the Cartel and Mafia stop at anything illegal.

Ashley flipped back to the medication section of Donna's chart. She cross-referenced the date of her son's visit. Her medication had been doubled and she had been almost comatose for six months immediately following that visit.

There were no therapy notes for the entire six months. There was no way of knowing for sure, but her son had probably told her about her father's suicide when he'd visited. It was odd that there were no therapy sessions if that were the case.

Ashley snapped more photos of the file contents before flipping back once more to the medical section. It provided Donna's date of birth, her birth parents' information, and various addresses where she'd lived. The chronological entries detailed her marriage to Lewis S. Fox and the birth of twin sons, one year later; one died at birth. She delivered at home with a physician and midwife on site. Dr. Edward Sloan signed the birth and death certificates of Donna's twins.

Over an hour later, Ashley looked up at the sound of the door opening and closing. "What did you come up with?" Chase asked.

She turned the chart around for Chase to see and pointed to the doctor signatures on the photo copies of the birth and death certificates. "Check this out."

"Holy shit! Why did the medical examiner deliver their children? And not just any medical examiner, but the one we indicted for falsifying autopsies and tampering with evidence in the last operation?"

"Yeah, the same bastard who removed bullets from dead cops and gave them to Fox to reload and reuse. It's not surprising; he was owned by Lewis Fox," Ashley said through clenched teeth as she snapped the last pictures and slammed the file shut.

"Send all those files to Anthony, now. They need that information before he and Drake interview Samuel," Chase said.

"I'll send them from the vehicle. Let's get the hell out of here now." She snatched up her purse and briefcase before heading out the door. Chase stopped briefly in the lobby and thanked the
personnel for their time, catching up with Ashley in the parking garage.

"You practicing for a marathon?" he asked as he unlocked the door to the SUV.

"No, just ready to get the hell away from this damn place." She opened the passenger door and climbed in, slamming the door behind her.

"Don't forget to send-"

"I'm sending them now." She took out her phone and began sending all the picture files to Anthony.

"Do you want to stop in Jacksonville and get something to eat before we get back on the plane?" Chase asked.

"Sounds good to me." Ashley stared out the window at the five o'clock traffic bottling up at the turnpike.

"It's going to be a bitch getting back on the interstate with all this traffic," Chase swore.

"Take the next right. It's a service road that goes along the inter-coastal waterway. It's about thirty miles longer but, in this traffic, will probably be quicker." She pointed ahead to the right.

"What the hell? It's got to be better than this bumper to bumper shit." He turned the wheel quickly to the right and veered off onto the service road.

Ashley retrieved her cell and tapped Anthony's name in her recent call log, waiting patiently for the call to connect. "Hey, babe, we're on our way to the airport in Jacksonville now. I sent you several picture files. You and Drake need to look at those before interviewing Samuel, if you haven't already. Love you." She slid the phone back in its case.

"I hope they get your message before talking to him." Chase frowned.

"Me too."

The sun had already set by the time they were nearing the Jacksonville airport exit. There had been very few cars on the inter-coastal so the drive had been nice. Ashley decided to call A.J. The phone rang and rang; she was just getting concerned when it was answered.

"Hey, Momma. Aunt Lynn said I could answer; she knew it was you."

"Hey, sweetie. What are you doing?"

"Uncle Morgan took me clamming and we gonna cook them tonight."

"That sounds good. Are you being good for Aunt Lynn and Brenda?"

"Yes, ma'am. Why are there a bunch of men here with us, Momma? We can't go nowhere without them." he. asked.

"They're just there to make sure you're safe while Mommy and Daddy are gone."

"Okay. Oh, Leo knocked Aunt Brenda off the deck this morning."

"Is she okay?" Ashley asked.

"Yeah, she fell in the sand. She was sweeping the deck and picked up Leo's Frisbee. He didn't mean to knock her off; he thought she wanted to play."

"I know. So long as no one was hurt, it's okay."

"Leo ran down the steps and kissed Aunt Brenda all over. He was sorry for knocking her down," he said.

"I'm sure he was, sweetheart." She laughed, picturing their German shepherd licking Brenda all over.

"Where's Daddy? Can I talk to him?"

"He's not with me right now, honey. I'm sure he will call you tonight."

"He called this morning. I just wanted to tell him about my clams." A.J. sounded disappointed.

"We'll both be home soon. I love you. I have to go now. Be good. Tell Uncle Morgan, Aunt Lynn, and Aunt Brenda I love them and will call later."

"I will. Love you, Momma. Tell Daddy I love him, too." A.J. hung up the phone and Ashley slid her finger across the screen, locking the device before sliding it back in the case. Hearing her son's voice had lifted her spirits.

"What the fuck?" Chase yelled just as the SUV lurched violently forward.

Ashley jerked around to see a large black van with tinted windows swerving from behind them only to be replaced by another just like it. She grabbed for her .45 but, before she could squeeze off a round, the van on the driver's side of the SUV crashed into them, pushing them off the roadway.

"Where the hell did they come from?"
The engine screamed as Chase dropped the accelerator to the floor and wrenched the wheel to the right.

"Dammit!" Ashley said, fumbling for her .45 as it slid just out of her reach. The SUV lurched violently.

"We're not going to make it, Ash!" Chase yelled.

Chapter 12

As the air bag engaged, Ashley felt the shoulder belt friction burn into her neck only seconds before they hit a power pole head-on. Ashley watched the hood of the SUV fold back into the windshield, shattering it before the momentum of the crash swung the top heavy SUV up and to the right. She heard an ear-piercing screech as they skidded along the concrete railing. The SUV flipped over the guardrail backward, and then it fell through the air. Chase screamed, "Open the door and jump!"

Ashley saw bright stars twinkling through the shattered windshield as her skull bounced off the headrest. The SUV hit the water with a thunderous splash. She felt like she'd been whacked from behind with a baseball bat. The cold, murky water quickly poured into the SUV. Definitely a lot faster than Ashley's brain could think what to do about it.

She tried to open the door, but it was too heavy, and by then, the water was up to her shoulders, and rising rapidly. She took a last gulp of air as it closed over her head. She couldn't see anything. The SUV seemed to spiral around and swing forward as it submerged. Finally, it came to a rest with one final jolt. Ashely couldn't tell if it was upside down.

Along with panic, she had now succumbed to a strange, sudden paralysis, and she couldn't feel her legs. *Should I try opening the door again?* she thought, and then realized the window was open. She tried to pull herself out of it, but couldn't. She was stuck. I'm going to die.

Ashley looked down and saw that she was still wearing her seatbelt. Gut-wrenching, nauseating pain tore through her right side as she desperately tried to unclip it. Her should was dislocated and shards of glass had punctured her chest.

She managed to pull herself through the window and gasped loudly as she broke the surface of the water. She quickly headed toward some mangroves growing from underneath the concrete road embankment to her left.

In her heavy boots, she was barely able to keep above water. When she was close enough to the shore to stand, she turned back toward where the SUV had gone under, in search of Chase. There was no sign of him. Did he make it out? God, I hope so.

The whole thing had happened at lightning speed. She headed out of the water through the seaweed and brush toward the road. "Dammit."

With its wall angled away from her, the embankment was going to be hard to climb. The top edge of the metal railing was about three feet over her head and her right shoulder was useless. It took Ashley three jumps off a large rotten tree stump to grab on. Because of the angle, she couldn't use her legs. As she dangled there, swinging back and forth, trying futilely to get her heavy-booted leg up onto the top, there was a splash behind her.

Please be Chase, she prayed.

"Ashley Cameron, or should I say Ashley Langston?" a creepily familiar voice called from the water's edge in a strangely calm manner. "How am I doing, you wanted to know?" he continued, as he sloshed through the water, closer and closer.

She started to cry in anger, pain, and frustration as she swung her leg up as hard as she could, managing to get the toe of her soaked boot onto the metal railing this time. But then it slipped off, and she was dangling there again helplessly as the splashing behind her got louder. She screamed as she tried again. Not even close. She was too terrified and hurt.

"Your arms aren't getting tired, are they?" Lewis Fox asked as he crashed through the brush behind her. "And what are you doing? Don't you know it's a crime to leave the scene of an accident?"

Her left arm was getting weaker. I have to try again. She swung up. And missed!

"Damn good try, Ashley. You almost had it that time." Fox clapped loudly from directly below as she swung back down.

Ashley kicked out blindly behind herself with all her strength. Her heavy boot heel came in direct contact with his face. There was a strangled scream, and he was on his knees, holding his busted and bleeding nose.

With the last bit of her strength, she did a chin-up to the rail. She hooked her right arm around it, feeling as if she'd torn her insides out as she rolled over the rail and fell into the roadway.

You have got to be fucking kidding me, she thought as she laid on her stomach with the blinding headlights of a van coming straight at her. There was nothing she could do, except watch the lights grow bigger and bigger.

She vaguely registered quick movement at the end of the guardrail.

"Fuck you!" Chase yelled as he unloaded his .45 into the side of the van. It careened off to the left, striking Chase and sending him over the edge like a ragdoll, before swerving right back toward her.

"Chase!" she screamed.

The van stopped eight feet in front of her with a loud squealing of brakes. From her view almost underneath the beastly rumbling vehicle, its grille looked as tall as the Eiffel Tower

"Get that goddamn bitch in the van!" Fox yelled from below.

She looked up seeing a middle-aged blond man, who looked extremely pissed-off. He reached down and drug her roughly to her feet.

"You stupid bitch," he said before drawing back and punching her in the face.

"You bastard." Ashley slithered to the hard pavement, the buzzing in her ears growing louder.

"How about you shut your face before I break those pretty cheekbones of yours?" he snarled.

Ashley looked over the concrete wall she'd just climbed and out toward the water's edge. She couldn't see anything. There was no movement in the brush or in the water. Please let Chase be okay and not dead.

Pain exploded in her head as Fox snatched her up by the hair and grinned. "Did you really think you could visit my wife undetected? I have been waiting for almost two years for this to happen. I knew eventually you would go see Donna." His voice was deeper now and ice cold.

"Fuck you." Ashley shouted.

"You know what I hate?" he asked, even colder sounding. "Hot little things like you who think that all they have to do in life is shake their tits and ass, and the world will be at their beck and call."

Fox pulled Ashley's face to within inches of his own, kissed her forehead, and then slammed the barrel of the gun hard into her skull. She felt dizzy; the surface of the road was coming up to consume her. The buzzing in her ears grew louder and louder, and then everything went fuzzy gray before going completely black.

Chapter 13

****

Off the Coast – Cayman Islands
Thursday Morning
10:00 a.m.

The Cessna Citation CJ4 was an impressive midsize jet with its 58" digitally pressurized cabin and cockpit. Anthony had just plugged his laptop into the seat monitor, surprised at the quietness of the cabin during flight. It seemed a shame that he, Brease, and Drake only occupied three of the six deeply cushioned, wide reclining leather seats.

"This is one more quiet ride," Anthony said.

"It's my favorite. I usually pilot, but I knew we needed to conduct a strategy plan. The CJ4 has a fifty foot wing span and requires only a little over 3,000 feet of runway. We can be 45, 000 feet in the air in 29 minutes. I wasn't sure what we would run into in the Caymans." Drake laughed.

"Samuel Fox is supposed to live in Grand Cayman. He has a place just west on Seven Mile Beach. North end of the beach, two hundred feet of waterfront at $10 million - just for the lot. There is a two story mansion on the property. I am sure we can't miss it. How long will it take?" Anthony asked, glancing at his watch.

"A little shy of two hours, provided the weather holds out. Sorry we were delayed leaving the airport. I'll speak to my crew about not having it fueled and ready to go. Didn't you tell me you guys lived in Costa Rica?" he asked.

"Yes, on the northeast - Caribbean side."

"Well, we'll only be about an hour and forty five minutes north – slightly east, if you want to stop and check on your boy before heading back," Drake said.

"Sounds like a plan. Wait until you meet him. He is a pistol," Anthony said, pride shining in his eyes.

"I can't wait."

"We just have to be very careful. Our home in Costa Rica's identity is totally protected and I want to keep it that way."

"No problem. The CJ4 is also equipped with a stealth exterior, making it undetectable to radar. She's the best!"

"Does she wash dishes and clean windows, too?" Anthony asked, laughing loudly.

"No, jackass, she doesn't. I need to check my incoming mail and see if we have anything relevant before we get there. The only drawback with this baby is you have to rely on the internal computer systems and radio due to her security features. Our cell phones don't work while in the cabin. That makes it impossible for anyone to ever track my location," Drake said, flipping his laptop open.

"I figured as much when I checked mine earlier and had no signal."

"They will work on the outside; you just have to be at least twenty five feet away from the plane."

"What about our laptops?" Anthony asked. "Can we use those inside the plane?"

"Yes. The plug-ins feed directly into my internal system, and it's a secure feed."

"Great. Where are we landing your baby?"

"A buddy of mine owns property near Seven Mile Beach. There is an old service road we will use for landing. It will be a few miles drive from there." Drake pushed a couple of buttons on the high frequency radio to make contact with his ground crew in the Caymans to alert them of his arrival.

Over an hour later, they hit major turbulence and had to fly around a large cell of thunderstorms. "How much time did we lose?" Anthony asked.

"About thirty minutes. We should still land within the hour." Drake glanced down at his watch and flipped his laptop closed.

"Are we close yet?" Brease asked, yawning slightly.

"Yes. Sleeping Beauty decides to rejoin us?" Drake asked.

"Stop staring at me," she whispered, embarrassed as she sat up.

He hadn't realized he'd been staring. Like a starving wolf who wanted to bite so badly he could taste it. Taste her.

She pulled her knees up and wrapped her arms around them in a protective manner.

"How much longer?" she asked.

Damn. Drake didn't let any expression cross his face. What the hell was wrong with him? She was the fiancé of Ashley's cousin and a member of the team. Those were lines you didn't cross. She was just so damn hot with those pouty lips and perky breasts. Drake quickly reined his emotions into check.

"We ran into some bad weather but we should be landing soon," he said.

Just as promised, an hour later the CJ4 was dropping altitude and soon coasting down a wide abandoned roadway. The plane taxied to the end of the dirt road, stopping next to a huge metal building. Drake pulled the door open and motioned for Brease and Anthony to follow. They climbed out of the plane. Drake went first, sweeping out with his weapon up. Anthony stayed by Brease.

Two black Range Rovers waited for them. Drake led them to the front one. After Anthony got in the back and Brease got in the front, Drake climbed into the driver's seat and slammed the door behind him. As soon as the Rover started moving, Drake opened the middle console and pulled out a cell phone.

"Alpha Two, the Mission is rolling," Drake said.

Brease glanced over and found Drake's eyes on her. Should a man's gaze really make you feel like you were on fire? His did. She looked away briefly and when she turned back toward him, he had the cell to his ear. They had just landed, so she couldn't imagine whom he was calling already. She looked away from him at the barren landscape that flew past. They passed miles of dry sand, marked occasionally by small palm trees struggling to survive.

"Damn!" Anthony exclaimed from the back seat.

"What's wrong?" Drake asked, tossing the cell back into the middle console.

"I left my cellphone on the charger in the plane," Anthony answered.

"You can use this one if you want to check on Ashley and Chase. It's a throw away. I keep one in all the vehicles we use."

"That's okay. I'll just check on them when we get back to the plane. Ashley would just get pissy anyway and accuse me of not believing she could do her job." He shook his head.

"We've hit Seven Mile Beach. Samuel's place should be about four miles up on the right," Drake said.

"How are we going to know Samuel when we see him if there are no pictures of him anywhere?" Brease asked.

"One of the guys in the Range Rover behind us is a local very rich business man, Lincoln Alvarez. He is going to go in under the pretense of seeking legal counsel. Once he meets with Samuel, he will leave and provide us with a detailed description," Drake answered.

"It doesn't seem possible that a wealthy lawyer has no media following. I can't believe the bureau couldn't find a single photo of him anywhere," Anthony said exasperated.

"Apparently he has several partners in his firm. The partners always handle all courtroom procedures and initial consults. My local guy will have to get through the partners first before he can meet with Samuel. He's the brains behind it all," Drake explained.

"So if Samuel can't meet with him today, we'll stay here until the meeting takes place?" Anthony asked.

"I have one last card to throw on the table. Brease, you'll accompany Lincoln."

"What the hell?" she squeeked.

"Why are we pulling in here?" Anthony asked, gesturing to the oceanfront cabin. "You said Samuel's place was four miles up."

"Come on, let's get out and go in," Drake commanded.

"I'm with Brease. What the hell?" Anthony said.

"You'll see shortly."

The trio entered the beach cabin followed by Lincoln Alvarez and his bodyguards. They were greeted by a pleasant middle-aged woman. She immediately took Brease by the arm and ushered her down the hall to the bedrooms while the remaining team waited in the living room.

Fifteen minutes later, Brease re-entered the room. Thick blonde hair framed her heart shaped face like a silk canopy, stopping short of the huge silver diamond hoop earrings dangling from her ears. Her plump bright red lips curved downward in displeasure. The scarlet red sheer halter-top scooped so low that it exposed all but the nipples of her double D breasts. A six carat diamond solitaire nestled just above her cleavage. Finely woven silk hose seamed up the back slid from beneath the short black and red ruffled miniskirt, all the way down to four inch black stiletto heels.

"That's the ticket," Drake replied.

"I look like a hooker!" Brease fumed.

"I don't know what to say." Anthony stood, staring open-mouthed.

"Based on the very limited intel we have... this is what Samuel goes for." Drake bowed toward Brease.

"I don't know if this is a good idea," Anthony warned.

"She is only accompanying Lincoln as his girlfriend. We've gathered enough intel to know that high profile cases are observed by Samuel via a two way mirror during consult. My hope is that he will be so enthralled by Chloe here..."

"That he will show his face?" Anthony interrupted.

"Exactly." Drake smiled.

"You guys can kiss my ass." Brease headed toward the bedroom.

"I'm not so sure this will work," Anthony said again.

The sharp dressed millionaire businessman stepped forward. "Please, ma'am. I will make sure no harm comes to you. My eighteen-year-old daughter got addicted to drugs when she got engaged to Samuel three years ago. I was always two steps behind them in my search for her. He kept her out of the country, jet-setting all over the world," Lincoln Alvarez pleaded.

"We can help you find her, but it doesn't have to be like this," Brease replied.

"You don't have to help me find her. She was dropped off on my front doorsteps six months ago, on her twenty-first birthday, stoned out of her mind.

She died within six hours from a cocaine overdose. Samuel discarded her like a worn out pair of shoes months before her death!" His voice quivered in pain.

"I am so sorry," Brease whispered.

"I have many regrets. My business enterprises kept me abroad most of her life. I was never there for her and her mother died in a plane crash when she was six." He hung his head in shame.

"I am so, so sorry," she repeated and gently touched Lincoln's shoulder.

"It's uncanny how much you look like her. She was so beautiful, young and full of life, before that vulture got his talons into her!" Lincoln frowned as he gently touched Brease on the cheek.

"Well, let's get this show on the road." She took his arm and they followed his bodyguards out to the vehicle.

"We won't let anything happen to you, Brease," Anthony whispered in her ear before closing the passenger door of their vehicle and getting in the Range Rover parked behind them.

"This will work. Brease is so damn hot. Samuel will come in his pants at first sight!" Drake said as he pulled the Range Rover onto the highway behind Lincoln Alvarez and Brease

"Did you know she looked like Alvarez's daughter?" Anthony asked.

"Just found out this morning, when I had them send me all the information they had acquired. I had the team work all day pulling this together. I felt that the resemblance would play in our favor," Drake answered.

"Nice work. By the way, I've seen the way you look at her. Just remember she has a fiancé, and he happens to be the Mayor of D.C. and my wife's cousin!" Anthony said.

Chapter 14

Chloe clung to Lincoln Alvarez like an adoring companion as they entered the exquisite law offices. "Mr. Alvarez, please be seated. Someone will be with you shortly," the receptionist said as she slid the glass door above the counter closed.

"Thank you," he replied, taking Chloe by the hand and ushering her to the plush white leather coach in the waiting room.

Within moments a young man approached the waiting couple. "If you will follow me, I'll show you to the law library. Your consultant will be with you soon."

Chloe stared at the floor to ceiling books filling the massive mahogany bookshelves lining two walls as they took the two seats opposite the marble topped desk. She noticed the large glass window was shrouded by rows and rows of hunter green silk on the opposite side of the desk and thought about how dark it was on the other side. She could see the window but nothing through it.

"Linc, I just love those green drapes. I want some for our beach house," she said in a sugary voice.

"Then you shall have them, my dear," Lincoln replied, picking up her hand and kissing the top ever so gently. She gave an exaggerated giggle, playing along with the charade.

They both turned in unison at the sound of the library door opening. "Good afternoon. I am Attorney Bourgnon. I will handle your consultation."

She looked up at the middle-aged man dressed in a navy blue Armani suite with a red silk tie winking discreetly beneath the lapels.

"I'm here to see Attorney Samuel Fox, not a junior partner. I was told he is the best and that is what I want. I mean you no disrespect. Money is no option," Alvarez stated emphatically.

"Just give me the specifics of your case and I will see if Attorney Fox is interested in being your lead counsel," Bourgnon replied.

Brease "accidentally" dropped the small black leather cigarette case onto the floor. She leaned forward directly in front of window and wet her dry red painted lips with the tip of her tongue. The six carat diamond solitaire dislodged itself from her large breasts and dangled in the air like a carrot.

"I will talk with no one but Fox," Alvarez replied again.

"I am sorry but that is not possible. The partners at this firm are all impeccably qualified and screen every client first. No one sees Mr. Fox any other way," Bourgnon informed him stoically, just as the intercom on the desk began to buzz softly. He lifted the phone to his ear.

"Yes, sir. I'll inform Mr. Alvarez."
Chloe glanced at Lincoln and tried to conceal her apprehension.

"That was Attorney Fox. If you will remain seated, he will be with you shortly." Bourgnon stood, quickly turned on his heel, and exited the room without a sound.

She wasn't sure if it was the thud of the door closing or her heart beating out of her chest. Her palms were sweaty and her mouth felt like she had just swallowed sandpaper. Lincoln Alvarez, sensing her nervousness, lifted her hand and began to gently massage her palm. He was just as nervous. Was he finally going to lay eyes on the man responsible for his daughter's death? Samuel had tossed her aside like a rag doll when he'd become bored with her. She had turned to drugs in her grief. Granted, it took her six months to commit suicide by overdose. Samuel Fox had no idea who he was; his wife had given birth to their child before they married and his own daughter had never carried his last name. Fox didn't even have the decency to attend her funeral. Lincoln was at a disadvantage; he had no idea what Samuel Fox looked like.

It seemed like an eternity before the heavy oak door gracing the law library entrance swung slowly inward. "Allow me to introduce myself. I am Attorney Samuel Fox." He extended his hand to Alvarez, never taking his steel gray eyes off Chloe.

She stared up at the tall muscular blond-haired man with a voice so mesmerizing that it was like spun silk. Was this really Samuel Fox?

He couldn't be more than twenty-six or twenty-seven. He was much younger than she had assumed, with his GQ hair shaved above the ears, slightly full and spiked on top and longer in the back. She had to admit, he was hot... in a roguish kind of way. He wasn't dressed like any lawyer she had ever seen, either.

This man was wearing a white button down collared shirt, the sleeves rolled up to the elbows, with a black leather vest buttoned up atop black tight fitting jeans. The crisp white linen shirt was unbuttoned to reveal fine curly hair over a golden tanned rippled chest. His strong chiseled features paled against the intensity of those steely eyes.

"Thank you for granting me a consult, Attorney Fox," Alvarez replied, completely emotionless.

"Business in a moment." Samuel dismissed Alvarez as he focused his attention completely on Brease.

"Hello." She didn't recognize her own voice. It came out so weak and strangled.

"And who might this delightful and vivacious looking creature be?" Samuel asked, taking her hand up to his lips, closing his eyes and breathing in her scent as his lips grazed her skin.

"This is my girlfriend, Chloe." Alvarez made the introduction.

"You are certainly a lucky man, Mr. Alvarez," Samuel replied.

"Thank you. Can we discuss the specifics of my case now?" He needed to get them out of here as quickly as possible.

"Soon. Very soon." Samuel walked around the desk like a panther before pushing the intercom button.

"Yes, Mr. Fox," a female voice answered immediately.

"Bring us refreshments in the law library.

Fresh fruit and my best bottle of champagne." He didn't wait for a reply.

"We just had lunch," Alvarez informed him.

"Nonsense. Indulge me with your presence." Samuel continued to devour Brease with his gaze.

She finally found her voice. "We have a prior engagement we're committed to attend within the hour."

Samuel leaned over and, with two slender fingers, lifted the solitaire diamond from between her breast and brought it to his lips before slowly releasing the gem. "I am in envy of your diamond. It has the sweetest home I have ever seen." He smiled, flashing perfectly white teeth.

"I, uh, I...." She stammered, finding no words.

"Sir, that is enough. I came here to seek legal counsel, not for you to maul my companion."

Alvarez took a step forward and pulled her to his side.

"I can't apologize for speaking the truth. Your companion is the most gorgeous woman I have ever laid eyes on." His gray eyes never left Chloe.

"You may be the best attorney in this area, but I will take my business and money elsewhere. Let's go, Chloe." Alvarez kept her protectively at his side as they headed toward the door. A young women entered, pushing a silver trolley laden with fruit and a bottle of champagne as they were exiting.

"Until we meet again," Samuel called out as he held his glass up for the young women to fill with the bubbly liquid.

Lincoln and Chloe wasted no time exiting the law firm and climbing into their awaiting vehicle to be chauffeured away.

"Chloe, I mean Brease, now that we are out of that awful lion's den, I can call you by your real name," he said compassionately.

"Yes," Brease answered, choking back the tears. She didn't know why she felt so violated.

Nelson, the chauffeur and bodyguard said. "I'm taking us to a beach house back in Grand Cayman. It has an underground garage. Drake and Anthony are waiting there for us to conduct a debriefing."

"Okay," Lincoln said quietly.

"We switched out our backup so as not to raise suspicion. The guys in the black charger behind us are part of our surveillance team." He floored the vehicle, veering onto the next interstate ramp for Grand Cayman. The drive was deathly silent. Neither Brease nor Lincoln felt like discussing Samuel Fox at the moment.

Less than an hour later, they were pulling into the underground garage with the steel door closing quickly behind their vehicle. Lincoln helped Brease out of the vehicle and up the three short steps. As soon as they entered the side door, Anthony and Drake both fired off the same question, "Did you meet Samuel Fox? What did he look like?"

"Yes, tall, blond, muscular... late twenties," she answered.

Tall, blond, and muscular could be anyone. Anthony offered her what he hoped was a smile.

"Do you remember his face well enough that you could probably talk to a sketch artist if we can get one here?

Get us a clear picture of him?" he asked. A crease appeared between Brease's eyes.

"We'll need to put it out on every law enforcement database, locally and abroad. That way we can find out if he has been involved in any illegal enterprises under an alias."

"A close image will also help us find out if this man is really Samuel Fox," Drake added.

She nodded and her lips twisted slightly. "I can do better than meet with your sketch artist." Her shoulders squared. "Give me a pencil and a piece of paper, and I'll draw the image for you."

Anthony tried not to let his satisfaction show. Brease was an artist; he remembered reading that in her bio. Sure, she usually worked with oils, but information indicated she could draw anything or anyone... in an instant.

"We'll want several sketches from different angles if you can?" he asked.

Now her shoulders straightened ever further back. "Will do."

"Hell, yes. This could be just the break we need." Drake smiled.

"I want those bastards caught. I want them stopped before they try a hit on my wife!" Anthony said with a vengeance. He knew the whole team felt the same way. They were not planning on backing off this operation, not until Lewis Fox and any other party involved was locked up or dead. It didn't really matter which. The mission wasn't over; in fact it might just be heating up.

Anthony looked down at her pale face.

"You look sick, Brease. Why don't you change and try to lie down for a while? You can take care of the sketches on the flight back home. We have a few details to iron out here before we can head back to the plane. The guards brought your clothes and put them in the bedroom down the hall. They will stay positioned outside your door so you don't have to worry," he said.

"Thank you. I have a fever and feel really sick to my stomach all of a sudden." She headed down the hall. She would be happy to shower off the filthy feeling she had from Samuel's brief touch and to get back into her real clothes. She was Brease, not Chloe.

Chapter 15

The team spent several hours reviewing all the information they had gained from the encounter with Fox's son, along with recent information from Drake's informant. Anthony sent one of the bodyguards out with a list of items they needed.

"Drake, I say we fly back to Florida this evening and return over the weekend to interview Samuel Fox. I think we would be better prepared after we circulate a sketch. I would like to see what comes out of the woodwork before we actually interview him," he suggested.

"I agree. The more ammunition we have, the better we can work it. You interview while I interrogate."

"You always did like the interrogation part of operations. I guess it will be like old times; I'm the good cop and you're the bad cop," he said, laughing.

Drake put his hand in the air and high fived Anthony. "You bet."

"Can you make arrangements to have part of your team here keep a tail on Samuel?" Anthony asked.

"Sure. I will make a call now."

"I just don't want him slipping away out of the country." Anthony said.

They loaded the Range Rover and prepared for the drive back to the airport while they waited for Brease to wake up. She had insisted on providing detailed information before becoming extremely nauseous and lying down. Lincoln went to the pharmacy owned by a friend of his and returned with nausea medication, which knocked her out. The operation had just begun and it was already taking a toll on her. She simply was not used to field work and had come down with a flu bug.

"We're finally going to know what Samuel Fox looks like," Anthony said with a smile.

"I told you this would work. Nothing like a hot woman to make a man lose his head. Especially one as hot as Brease."

"Are you sure this damn cell works?"

"You got it out of the console, right?" Drake asked.

"Yeah," he replied, punching numbers into the phone once more.

"It works. Why?"

"I have been trying Ashley and Chase for over two hours and it keeps going straight to both of their voicemails. I've left several messages and no return calls from either of them yet. They should have already been on the road back to the airport in Jacksonville by now."

"Maybe they're somewhere with limited cell service or they stopped to get something to eat," Drake suggested.

"You could be right. If I don't hear back from them by the time we get to the plane, I'll call Roberto and see if he or Grayson has heard from them." Anthony slipped the cell into his pocket.

"One of you should have woken me up," Brease said as she walked into the den, dropping her bag on the floor.

"We took advantage of the time and reviewed all the information we have so far. Is the stomach ache gone?" Anthony asked.

"Almost. I am just ready to get out of here."

"Then let's getting moving and grant the lady's wish." Drake smiled, retrieving her bag from the floor.

"I can get that," she said.

"I got it. What do you have in here anyway? Rocks?" he asked with a laugh.

"Just my laptop, a couple of guns, and boxes of ammo. I'm wearing the clothes and shoes that were in there."

"A lady after my own heart." He chuckled, opening the door for Brease to follow Anthony out to the SUV.

"You can ride shotgun. I'll get in the back," Anthony told her as Drake climbed in the driver's seat.

"Okay. How long did you guys let me sleep? It's already dark."

"You were out for a little over three hours. I got you a drawing pad and a pack of drawing pencils while you were napping." Anthony passed the bag up to her.

She opened the plastic bag and examined the pencils. "These will work great."

"How long does it take you to sketch a person in detail?"

"Once we get on the plane and get airborne, I can have one complete within an hour or so. I'll do several."

"Great," he said, pulling the cell out of his pocket and redialing. Still no answer on Ashley's phone. No answer on Chase's phone. "Dammit, what the hell are they doing?"

Drake looked in the rearview mirror at Anthony. "No answer yet?"

"No. I can't check the messages on my cell because it's on the plane. I'm calling Roberto."

"What's going on?" Brease asked.

"Anthony has been trying to get up with Ashley and Chase going on three hours now," Drake replied.

"Oh, no."

"Roberto, Anthony here. Have you heard from Chase or Ashley?"

"Nope, and I have been trying to get up with Chase for about two hours now," Roberto answered.

"We've got agents in Jacksonville, right?" Anthony asked.

"Yes. I talked to the pilot who flew them over there along with the DEA agent. They're both still standing by at the plane, waiting for them to get back. As of about fifteen minutes ago, they hadn't arrived yet."

"When was the last time you talked to one of them?"

"A little before 10 a.m. this morning. They had left the airport in the SUV and were headed to the psychiatric hospital in New Haven. Chase just called to check-in," Roberto said.

"Okay, they should have been there by noon at the latest. Even if they were there a couple of hours and stopped to eat somewhere, we should have heard from them by now. It's eight o'clock at
night. They were less than three hours from the airport."

"I'll send the agent from the airport to trace their route and see if he comes up with anything. In the meantime, I'll contact one of the CIA guys near there and see if there are any unusual reports, accidents or anything."

"Okay. Just be very limited with any information you give out. Receive information – don't give any. I don't care how long you've known him. We trust no one outside our immediate team right now. Drake, Brease, and I will fly toward Jacksonville. We should be at the airport down here in about ten minutes. If you hear anything, notify me immediately. Go ahead and inform Director Madison." Anthony disconnected the call.

"Change of plans?" Drake asked.

"We need to head toward Jacksonville, not the safe house." Anthony snapped.

"I'm sure everything is fine. Chase and Ashley are both great agents."

"Those two can handle anything," Brease added.

"Just get us to your jet as quickly as possible, Drake. I can find Ashley's location from there," Anthony mumbled.

"Okay." Drake gave him a puzzled look before flooring the Range Rover.

Chapter 16

The speeding Range Rover covered the rutted path in record time. Drake opened up its three-hundred horsepower engine full throttle on their way back to the airport. Brease boarded first and immediately began pulling out the pencils and sketch pad. Anthony tossed his bag and briefcase quickly onto the leather seat inside the plane.

"Drake," he called as he headed back out of the plane, "hook up my laptop and get it running. I'm going to step outside and check my cell."

"Will do. I'm going to try Roberto again from the radio."

Anthony walked about thirty feet from the plane before tapping the cell phone screen to retrieve his messages. He listened. "Hey, baby, it's Ash. I sent you a bunch of files to your email. You need to take a good look at these before you and Drake interview Samuel.

I just can't believe this shit. Chase and I are leaving the hospital now. I tried you earlier and couldn't get through. Will try again later and explain. Love you."

Anthony replayed the message again. She'd left the message shortly after five. "Love you too, baby," he whispered to the cell phone, squeezing his eyes tightly shut for a few seconds before walking back toward the plane.

"Anthony, get up here now," Drake hollered from the steps of the plane.

Anthony ran the few feet to the entrance. "What is it?"

"I just got off the radio with Roberto. The CIA just called him back and there was a report of an automobile accident just south of Jacksonville. They have one survivor in critical condition transported to Jacksonville Medical Center." He spoke quickly.

"Is it Ashley?"

"No. The description fits Chase," Drake said solemnly.

"Where the hell is Ash?" Anthony demanded. "I told you all she didn't need to go on this operation. Operation Crossroads? Crossroads to Hell is what it is," he shouted.

"The CIA has operatives canvassing the area of the accident. Apparently the SUV went off in the water. Roberto will contact me back as soon as he knows anything. He and Grayson are on a private plane to Jacksonville now."

"Did you get my laptop hooked up?" Anthony asked, shoving past Drake.

"Yes. It's on now. What are you looking for?"

"Two things. Ash left me a message shortly after five. She and Chase were leaving the hospital and she sent files to me that she wanted us to look at before we interviewed Samuel." He keyed in his password as he spoke.

"Okay. You said two things?

"You remember the Rolex I gave her?"

"Yeah. What does that have to do with anything?"

"It's equipped with a GPS tracking device, the best you can get. It will give me her exact location down to twenty five feet proximity."

"Ashley will kill you for putting a GPS device on her," Brease said, lifting her head momentarily from the sketches.

"I just hope she is alive to kill me," Anthony said, his voice cracking slightly with emotion. He pulled up the software for the GPS tracking system and they sat back watching the snowflake shape icon spinning around and around as it searched for coordinates.

"Why is it taking so long?" Drake asked after a few minutes.

"I don't know. I hope she still has the watch on. You said there was an accident?"

"Yes, near the intercostal waterway just south of Jacksonville. FHP is working the accident. The guardrail was all bent up so they believe a vehicle went over into the water. The male body recovered, we believe, is Chase."

"Have they requested a dive team? How far are Roberto and Grayson from Jacksonville?"

"A dive team is en route and Roberto and Grayson should be there by 10:00 at the latest," Drake said, looking at his watch.

"How quick can you get us there?"

"About 10:30."

Anthony flipped back to the emails he had just opened while waiting for the GPS software to supply the correct coordinates.

He and Drake quickly scanned through all the documents sent. "This makes no damn sense. Why did Sloan deliver Donna's twins at their home?"

"He also signed the death certificate for the twin who was born dead," Drake said.

"Sloan was the medical examiner for years, so signing death certificates wouldn't be unusual."

"He's the one you put in prison based on the information from FBI Director Lawrence's suicide note, right?" Drake asked.

"Yup, so why would he deliver Donna and Lewis Fox's children at their home?'

"Okay, now Donna was the daughter of the director of the FBI, and she married Lewis Fox, the leader of the Dixie Mafia. The scarf that Ash received had an "F" monogrammed on it but the DNA was that of Ricky Martinelli, son of Adrianno Martinelli – Colombian Drug Lord.

Right?" Drake confirmed, trying to decipher the importance of the files Ashley had sent them.

"Right, so why would Ashley be so adamant that we needed to review this information before interviewing Samuel?" Anthony mused.

"I don't know."

"And Ricky Martinelli is dead. Ashley killed him…"

"There has to be something we're missing," Drake said, puzzled.

"Okay, coordinates are coming up. 4544 Oceanside Lane, Jacksonville, Florida."

Drake slid the door open between the cockpit and cabin. "Key in 4544 Oceanside Lane, Jacksonville, Florida and land us as close to that location as possible," he instructed his pilot.

"Okay, according to the property appraisal website for Jacksonville, 4544 Oceanside Lane is a business. The Players' Lounge," Anthony said.

"What the hell? Why is Ashley in a bar?"

"Property taxes are paid by DM Holdings Company."

"What kind of place is this lounge? I've never heard of it."

"Tax records on it only go back two years. Let me pull it up on the internet and see what information it gives us." Anthony quickly entered the information and waited for a response. "Strip club featuring exotic dancers and live bands nightly, open seven days a week."

"Go back to the property appraisal website," Drake said.

"Okay." Anthony clicked back over to the website.

"Pull up the building information."

"It's a two story building with an unfinished basement. Concrete structure, ten thousand square feet. Five thousand upstairs and five thousand downstairs. Downstairs includes… it looks like a four car garage was added on to the east side of the basement area."

"A DM Holdings Company," Drake said.

"Dixie Mafia!" They realized at the same time.

"Lewis Fox has Ashley!" Anthony shouted.

"That still doesn't explain the contract hit on her by a dead man. Your team did double check the DNA on that scarf, right?" Drake asked.

"Yes, twice. The DNA belonged to Ricky Martinelli."

"Maybe this will help. It's a little rough, but I was trying to get it done as quickly as possible." Brease handed Anthony and Drake her first completed sketch.

"You're shitting me." Anthony stared down at the sketch.

"Is there something wrong? I did it quickly. I'm sorry. I'll do another one with more detail."

"This is fucking Ricky Martinelli!" Anthony said.

"Anthony. Think about it. That's what Ash was trying to tell us. That is the connection. Director Madison said, during the debriefing, that he was going to the hospital to wait for Director Jones to be able to speak so he could find out the connection between the Dixie Mafia and the Colombian Drug Cartel," Drake said.

"Yeah, so?"

Drake thumped the sketch with his finger. "This is not Ricky Martinelli, it is Samuel Fox… Ricky's twin brother. The twin wasn't born dead. Dr. Sloan was owned by the Dixie Mafia and he forged that death certificate. Fox gave Martinelli one of his sons to raise as his own. That formed the alliance between the Mafia and the Cartel."

"Oh, my God. Fox took the hit out on Ashley because she killed his son," Anthony said in shock.

"Twins carry the same DNA. The lab would have needed to run additional tests to break down the mitochondrial DNA." Drake said.

"Oh, hell. He will definitely kill her." Anthony said.

"The chances are 10 billion to 1 of two people having the same DNA. It only comes into play with identical twins. The basic DNA would have come back to the only hit in the system, which was Ricky Martinelli. Samuel Fox has never been arrested, so his DNA is not on file. Fingerprints would have been the only distinctive difference," Drake elaborated.

"I'm telling you, Fox will kill Ashley. We have to get to her now, that bastard is nothing but pure evil." Anthony said, devastated.

"Okay. Let me think. I am going to make a few radio calls to my team back in the Caymans. I'll have them kidnap Samuel Fox and put him on a plane headed to Jacksonville. We may need him as leverage; I'm worried we can't get to Ashley in time. If we contact the Players' Lounge and get word to them that we have Samuel Fox and we're going to kill him if they don't release Ashley, it may buy some time."

"Do it. I bet Ashley figured it out," Anthony said.

"I'm going to radio Roberto and see if he has any more information on Chase and see who we have in the field that might be closer to Jacksonville." He contacted the safe house team.

"Roberto, Anthony here. Any news?"

"I was just about to call you. I just hung up with the CIA Agent in charge in Jacksonville. A couple of the CIA guys made it over to Jacksonville Medical Center. Chase is there, in surgery now. He's busted up pretty bad, several cracked ribs with one of them puncturing a lung. Both of his legs are broken and he has a busted skull. He is in very critical condition and may not make it through surgery. I got up with Madison and he's making arrangements to get Brenda and their son flown up to Jacksonville. We've got a six man team about ten minutes from the Player's Lounge now. If you need them to go on in…they can. We're still about an hour away. How far out are you guys?" Roberto asked.

"At least another hour, hold off on letting that team go in alone… it would be an ambush." Anthony said.

"I asked the CIA team to pull covert surveillance and provide an update before moving in," Roberto said.

"Okay, we'll have Samuel in custody shortly and they'll be flying him toward Jacksonville too, just in case we need him as leverage to get Ashley out of there alive," Anthony informed Roberto.

"Okay, touch base with you guys shortly."

Chapter 17

****

Somewhere outside of Jacksonville, Florida
Thursday Night
10:00 p.m.

Ashley had no idea how long it had been when she finally woke up. She didn't open her eyes right away. As always over the last ten years, she sat still, held her breath with eyelids shut, momentarily unsure and afraid of where she'd find herself. Aching all over, Ashley's memory was coming back; the last thing she remembered was being thrown in the back of a van.

She slowly opened her eyes. She was cold and her clothes were wet. *Where was she?* Ashley felt like a band of drummers were auditioning inside her head.

Adjusting her eyes to the dimly lit room, she could tell it was in a basement. It was cold, damp, and smelled like decomp and stale whiskey. She could hear music playing overhead.

She was strapped to a large wooden chair in the middle of the room. There were small electrodes taped to her chest, upper arms, and legs with wires going to a large machine about two feet away. Ashley tried to move and wrench her arms free but the leather bands were tight and unbreakable. She was bound by a leather strap around her waist and ankles. Tears filled her eyes as I looked down at the cracked face on the watch Anthony had given her. She scanned the room in fear. Oh, my God, this was it… she was going to die here. She would never hug her baby boy again or hear his beautiful laughter. She would never see Anthony's smile again...

A shadowy figure emerged from across the room. Ashley squinted her eyes as the basement was flooded with bright lights. The pain in her head was almost unbearable as she opened her eyes wider to focus on the figure. It was Lewis Fox.

"I see you finally came to?"

"Why am I here?"

"So I can kill you, slowly, and watch you suffer." He laughed.

"Fuck you. I hope you burn in Hell."

"Now that is no way to greet an old friend." He smiled, stepping closer.

"You're no friend. You are a murdering bastard. What did you do with my partner?"

"After he tried to shoot us, we ran him over and left him for dead."

"Why are you doing this?"

"You mean you don't know? You didn't get all the answers you wanted when you visited my wife?" he asked.

"I don't know what you're talking about."

"Do you deny that you went to see Donna?"

She licked my dry busted lips, tasting blood inside her mouth. "I went to see her to find you."

"All of you cops are so predictable. I knew you would eventually show up. What did you hope to learn from her? I have taken extreme measures over the years to ensure that she would never be able to turn evidence against me. I've always been at least one step ahead of the cops." Fox spit at her before continuing.

"That includes making sure her healthcare providers use the oldest and most damaging antipsychotic medications possible. I am that hospitals largest contributor." Fox gave a wicked laugh.

"I went to find out why you took out a contract on me for one," she managed to spit out.

"You're not that stupid, now, are you? You bitch, you murdered my son! For that you have to pay," he said through clenched teeth.

"I didn't kill your son." Ashley was trying to stall.

"Ha, ha, ha… this stupid act doesn't become you. You murdered my son, Ricky Martinelli."

"But, but… Ricky Martinelli was Adrianno's son, not yours… Oh, my God." She opened her eyes wide, attempting to fake astonishment before continuing. "Your twins… they both lived! You had Medical Examiner Stone falsify the death certificate and gave one of them to Adrianno. That is how you gained control of the Colombian Drug Cartel."

Fox brought his hands up and slapped them together three times. "I applaud your powers of deduction, Mrs. Langston."

"The DNA… on the scarf that you sent me was really that of your son, Samuel…"

"Very good. It took you long enough to put the pieces together."

If she could just keep him talking… she continued. "They were identical twins so the DNA profiles would have been exactly the same. You were very careful to make sure there were no fingerprints because I'm sure you know that identical twins will have very similar contours and ridges in their fingerprints but they will not be the same. You see, even though identical twins are genetic duplicates, the shape of their fingerprints are not solely linked to genes. We would have figured it out sooner had there been fingerprints." Ashley knew she was rambling… trying to buy time. She had already figured out that Ricky was his son.

"It was the perfect plan. I gained ultimate control and Adrianno acquired a son as his wife could not conceive. Adrianno was a fucking idiot to have hired a damn CIA man. He should have known Victor Shayne was actually your husband, Anthony Langston." Fox said smugly.

"Did Donna know?" Did she know you gave away your own flesh and blood to control a drug empire?" Ashley asked.

"You sure are a nosy bitch for someone about to die. But I'll humor you for a while. Donna didn't know until my weak ass son went to see her and told her. It cost me a fortune to remove the information from Donna's hospital file. I kept the wrong son. Samuel is a pussy. He didn't know he had a twin brother until I took him to the funeral. You should have seen the look on his face when he saw himself dead in a casket. They looked exactly alike even though they were raised a world apart."

"How could you be so heartless?" She tried to suck air into her lungs as the room began to spin.

He stepped to within an inch of her face and whispered in her ear, "Don't worry, Ashley Langston. You know the truth now and your husband isn't here to save your ass. After I make you suffer for a long time, I will kill him just like you killed my son. A life for a life."

With much resolve, Ashley ignored the pounding in her head and quickly jerked her mouth around, catching Fox's ear in her teeth. She bit down as hard as she could, ripping a piece of flesh from his ear and spit it out on the concrete floor.

He screamed before backhanding her across the face. "You fucking bitch." He pulled a handkerchief from his pocket and held it to the left side of her face. "I see you looking closely at my handkerchief. Do you want to look at the monogram?" Fox shoved the bloody piece of linen in her face.

"Don't turn your face away. It's just like the one I sent you."

"Burn in hell, Fox." Ashley yelled.

"Take a good long look at the chair you are sitting in, bitch. This is my newest invention. It's my adaptation of an electric chair. You see, there is just enough current on the lower settings to cause excruciating pain. Your body will accept the shocks and convulse violently, without causing death. Once you recover from the initial shock, I will increase the levels. At the highest level, your blood vessels will begin to burst as your body convulses even more and more violently, and then the brain damage will begin. You will start bleeding from your nose and then your mouth, before you smell your flesh burning.

Ready to have some fun?" He snapped his right

fingers loudly over his head.

"You fucking bastard."

"Pull the switch down," he commanded someone Ashley couldn't see.

Ashley screamed out in pain as electric shocks coursed through her body. Her whole body convulsed and jerked in the chair for what seemed like an eternity before her head fell forward as everything went black.

"If I leave here tomorrow, would you still remember me..." Ashley heard the piano fading in the distance and a male voice singing the old rock song, "Freebird." *Am I dead?* She listened to the music drifting down from overhead for a few more seconds before cautiously opening her eyes. Her head was splitting; she was bleeding, and hurt everywhere. She tried to focus her eyes by blinking several times. The only thing on the concrete wall in front of her was a Coors Light sign, flashing on and off in neon blue. The digital clock attached read 10:00 p.m.

Ashley felt dizzy. The dirty concrete floor seemed to ripple upward. Her stomach began to clench tightly. After a moment, she realized it was full blown nausea caused by pain, anger and terror. The contents of her stomach started to slosh and turn, demanding immediate release.

"Hey, bitch, anything else you want to know before we have some more fun? I'll tell you anything, because you won't be leaving here alive." Fox stepped into view, snapping and clicking the camera held in his hand. The bright flash from the camera blinded her momentarily.

"Th.. the team, will k… kill you." Ashley weakly muttered.

Fox laughed loudly. "So, what do you say we do some close-up head shots? I want to remember these next few hours forever." He snapped more pictures.

"Humor me… I want a picture of each stage of your slow and tortured death. I will make copies and send them to your husband daily before I kill him." Fox laughed loudly.

I turned and heaved loudly and violently onto Fox's shoes. He howled in disgust before raking the barrel of a gun hard across my lips and teeth.

"Fuck you." Ashley weakly spit blood on the floor.

"Ha, ha, ha… Time for some more shock therapy, I'd say."

"You said we would ta,,, talk." Ashley held her breath in the silence that followed. Trying to think of anything to stall Fox.

"You realize how close you are to losing your life?"

"If you kill m... me, there will be no... nowhere for you to h... hide. The team will cross roads to Hell to hunt you down." It took all Ashley could do to speak.

"Your team couldn't find an elephant in the middle of an empty ballfield." He laughed again before snapping his fingers. "Crank the power up to level 2."

Ashley dug her fingernails into her palms and braced herself for the shock.

Chapter 18

****

Private Airstrip - Jacksonville, Florida
Thursday Night
10:20 p.m.

The plane grunted and groaned loudly as it bumped to a stop on the makeshift runway.

"Here take these. Unlock it." Drake tossed keys to Anthony as they jumped from the plane the minute the door fell downward. He pointed to the Jeep parked on the runway next to two SUVs.

"Throw our gear in the Jeep. We're about Ten minutes from the Players' Lounge. I'll check in with Roberto for updates," Anthony said.

"I've got the computer equipment," Brease told them as she climbed in the back of the Jeep. Drake threw duffle bags full of weapons and ammo into the back beside Brease and climbed into the driver's seat. He floored the Jeep and followed the six member team of agents standing by waiting for them to arrive.

The convoy sped away from the airport at lightning speed as the salty sea-air filled the interior of the Jeep. Anthony pulled the radio from the middle console. "Berto, you got it on?"

"Go ahead. We just set up at an abandoned warehouse about a block up from the Lounge."

"Drake, Brease, and I've just left the airport. We're following some agents over to the Players' Lounge."

"Okay. What's the plan?" Roberto asked.

"We're going to bust in through the garage on the east side of the basement beneath the club. That is the only access we have been able to locate. We enter from the east. They should be holding Ashley on the east side of the building."

"We've been monitoring traffic coming and going for the past fifteen minutes. There has been quite a bit of movement. The upper parking garage is filled with patrons of the lounge," Roberto said.

"I figured as much. If we blow out the bottom, we run the risk of the whole place collapsing and killing a bunch of innocent people. Dammit. I'll get right back to you."

"Check with my crew and see how far behind us they are," Drake said, swerving quickly to the right and tailing the SUVs in front of him.

"Alpha One to Delta Two," Anthony repeated twice.

"Delta Two, go ahead, One."

"How long before you're here with your cargo?" Anthony asked.

"About..." Delta Two's radio faded out.

"Delta Two, try it again. Your radio signal faded."

"Two minutes from landing. Repeat, two minutes from landing."

"Bring your cargo to the abandoned warehouse next to the lounge. Set up the camera feed and contact me immediately on my cell phone once mission accomplished," he ordered.

"10-4. Out."

"God, I hope Ashley is okay."

Drake glanced over. "We'll get her out of there."

Brease reached up and lightly touched Anthony on the shoulder. "She's going to be okay."

He stared out into the dark night, reflecting on the past few years of his life. He had lost Ashley once because of Lewis Fox and Adrianno Martinelli. They had found each other again and were living a good life, raising their son. With the Cartel leaders eliminated, he'd felt a little more at peace. However, he had always known the day would come when they would face Fox again.

Anthony saw the neon red flashing sign, "Players' Lounge," flashing just ahead at the next crossroads.

"Next Crossroads is the entrance to Hell," he stated solemnly.

"The other teams are just arriving on site and ready to penetrate. No time like now to bust Hell wide open," Drake replied.

Six vehicles raced down the ramp to the lower level parking. Agents in vests and shields exited quickly and flooded the exterior of the west wall of the garage. With the first penetration of the block wall garage, the work of the demolition crew consumed each member of the team.

Whatever their private fears, they were professionals and the life of a team member inside the basement demanded their expert and precise attention.

"Brease, you stay with the Jeep and monitor radio traffic. Go ahead and update Director Madison of the situation here," Anthony commanded as he and Drake exited the vehicle.

The demolition crew pulled tools out of the duffle bag in rapid speed. Platinum drills made quick work, knocking a hole into the exterior of the block garage wall. They concentrated on the exterior wall to avoid collapsing the whole building. The disciplines of basic precautions were swiftly consigned to aggravating nuisances as it took less than a full four minutes to gain entry. It was thirty five minutes after ten when Drake signaled the fire call. The alarm began squealing loudly, sending Cartel henchmen fleeing from the building.

The first one of them stepped out onto the concrete pad, adjacent to the garage area, assault rifle poised in midair. Somewhere between the busted entrance and the cement pad, he had his stomach ripped open with a blade so long it cut deep enough for backbone cartilage to protrude through spinal lacerations. He fell silently into a pool of warm blood, followed quickly by four more Cartel men in the same manner.

"I've got your back. Get in there and get Ashley. We'll take out the rest of them, and be in as quick as we can." shouted Drake, swinging his military machete quickly to the demise of two other Mafia bodyguards.

A black Mercedes quickly appeared, blocking the exit from the underground garage. A quick assessment alerted the team that it was one of the Mafia's henchmen. They had to act quickly or he would alert Fox. Roberto and Grayson ran quickly up the sloping driveway of the basement of the garage and yanked the door of the Mercedes open just as Drake arrived. Drake registered the startled look on the face of the driver, just as the man reached over across the seat for a transistor radio.

In the next few seconds, Drake witnessed one of the quickest assassinations he had ever seen. Grayson reached under his jacket, revealing a very large holster, and pulled out a Smith and Wesson 500 .50 Cal. Magnum, with a huge silencer on the end. He held the gun up with both hands, and fired one shot right into the driver's head. His head completely exploded and disintegrated all over the dashboard and front seat of the car. The driver's body slumped over in the front seat. Drake reached over him and retrieved the radio before closing the car door almost casually.

They rounded the corner of the break in the building and headed in to help Anthony. Halfway across the garage, Roberto pointed toward the corridor. A dark-haired, heavy-set man stood guarding the entrance to the adjacent room. He held an AK-47 in his right hand and a similar radio in his left hand.

Drake put up finger up to his lips and motioned for Roberto and Grayson to take cover as he pulled out the radio he'd removed from the Mercedes. He lifted it as unobtrusively as possible to the side of his head and pressed the oblong button in, holding it down. There was a brief blare of static before he quickly adjusted the volume.

"Get out back, now," Drake said over the radio.

"10-4." The heavyset guard, hearing the command on his radio, ran toward the rear parking garage. Just as he rounded the corner, Drake kicked the gun from his right hand and slit the guard's throat with the end of his machete, almost decapitating him in one fluid movement.

A quick horrible sound emerged from the guard's throat before he slid lifelessly down the side of the concrete wall onto the ground below.

"Grab his radio," he commanded Grayson.

Screams could be heard from overhead. The bar civilians were reacting to the fire alarm and evacuating in a panic.

They had to get in to help Anthony. Leaving the remaining team members behind, Drake, Roberto, and Grayson reached the basement door and listened briefly, before quietly entering the room. Anthony pushed through the concrete building pieces and made his way to the corridor leading over to the room adjacent to the garage area, and eased across the room to a crouching position behind Fox.

Cold-blooded, killing-on-his-mind rage surged through Anthony at the sight of Ashley tied to a chair in the center of the room, head hung down, bleeding, lifeless, and unmoving. Fox was leaning over her.

"It's over Fox. Step the fuck away from her now or I will blow your fucking head off." Anthony commanded, as his right hand reached for his weapon.

Fox spun away from Ashley and sprang into a fighting stance. "I wouldn't pull that weapon, if I were you. And, you weren't invited to the party yet. I didn't plan to extend your invitation until tomorrow. How the fuck did you find us tonight?" A knife glinted faintly in his hand.

Blood roared in his ears and Anthony didn't mess around with any finesse moves. He moved to charge forward. "It doesn't matter how I found you, you bastard. You won't leave here alive."

"I wouldn't do that if I were you. You see that window back there? One of my men is in that room and he controls the electrical current flow to your little wife here. I can fry her in a second." Fox laughed.

"You fucking bastard."

Fox snapped his fingers. "Give them a little demonstration."

Anthony watched as Ashley's head jerked up and her body thrashed and convulsed against the restraints in the chair. His heart stopped as she screamed out in pain.

"What do you want, Fox?"

"What do I want? Well, let me see. I want my dead son back. Can you do that for me, Anthony?"

"No but I can call off the murder of the son you have remaining," he said flatly.

"You lying piece of shit. He has nothing to do with my business enterprises. He doesn't have the balls for it, too much like his mother. I should have known FBI blood would have tainted my children. Ricky was tough like me."

"Let's just test your theory, why don't we, Fox?" Anthony pulled his cell phone out, tapped the screen a couple of times, and stepped to within
inches of Fox before turning the screen toward him. Fox glared at the screen of the phone as he saw the recorded video of his son, sitting in a chair with a large caliber weapon held to his temple.

"If you're listening to this," he said, "I have been kidnapped. Not that you give a shit; you never have. I ask you, as your son, to put an end to your vendetta. I've watched my whole life as you destroyed me and my mother. I never even knew that I had an identical twin brother until you felt the need to drag me to his funeral and show me his dead lifeless body inside a damn casket. Did you ever stop to think what that would do to me? It was like seeing myself dead. You never had time for me, just threw money at me to keep me entertained and out of your hair. I made it through law school and passed the bar with the highest honors in my class. You didn't even come to my graduation. I have made a successful career as a lawyer and distanced myself from your business enterprises, as you call them, when in reality it's just Mafia and Cartel disorganized crime. Your blood money gained from drug, gun, and sex trafficking have brought my mother and me to the crossroads of Hell. You locked her away and had her medicated so you didn't have to deal with her. I quit taking your money years ago. I don't know why I am bothering to plead with you now. My blood on your hands won't make any more difference to you than all the other contract hits you've executed. What's it going to be, Dad?"

"You bastards. Let my fucking son go now, or I will execute your bitch immediately." Fox snarled at Anthony.

Anthony tapped the screen on the phone again. "Convert to the live feed, he commanded.

"Fuck you. You don't have the balls to kill my son." Fox took a step, closing the distance between them.

Anthony had to think fast. Trying to shoot Fox wouldn't work... he had to distract him and close in on him.

"Here, this is for you." He tossed the phone to Fox hoping this would distract him briefly.

Fox caught the phone with one hand. "Dad, end... end this n... now."

"An eye for an eye, Fox. It's too late. You kill my wife and you can watch as your son's brain splatter the wall behind him."

With sudden unexpected movements, Fox dropped the phone onto the floor and lifted his left hand, snapping his fingers in the air, while using his right hand to extract a large automatic from the belt holster under his jacket. The second his arm began to descend from his side, Anthony lunged with all his weight, jabbing him in the ribs. The two men wrestled. Anthony charged forward and grabbed Fox's wrist, throwing his shoulder into his chest, before slamming him into the concrete wall behind them.

"Stay to the left." Drake hollered at Anthony as the team took out four Mafia guards that were leveling their weapons on Anthony.

Anthony and Fox wrestled fiercely as a spray of bullets sped past them, shattering and splintering the room behind them. Drake and the team effectively executed the controller and three more Fox henchmen.

Fox's whole face contorted spastically. A sound of gurgling blood erupted from Lewis Fox twisted mouth. Anthony felt the burst of warm blood exploding around his hand as he looked down at the long switchblade he held. He had ripped Fox's stomach open from pelvis to ribcage.

"Throw down your weapons and hit the fucking floor, now!" Drake commanded the Mafia men left standing.

Drake, Roberto, Grayson, and the rest of the team secured the remaining Mafia henchmen and guards. Anthony released Fox and his dead body slid to the concrete floor in a heap. He ran over to Ashley, slumped over in the chair unmoving. "Ashley, honey, are you all right?"

She remained slumped over, ghostly pale, bleeding from the mouth and unmoving. "It's okay, baby. I'm here." He undid her and lifted her lifeless body, cradling her gently in his lap.

"Talk to me, baby. Please say something. Fox is dead; he can't hurt you ever again," Anthony begged as he stroked her hair away from her face and kissed her on the cheek.

"I've already called the medics; they should be here any second," Drake said.

"I can't lose her now. She's my whole world," he replied, tears rolling down his cheeks as he cradled Ashley close to his chest. "She's not breathing, she's not breathing…"

He laid her softly onto the floor and tilted her head back. Gently pinching her nose closed, he took a deep breath and covered her mouth with his
before breathing several deep breaths into her body. He placed his ear over her chest and listened briefly before repeating the resuscitation techniques again and again. Anthony lifted his head between breaths to watch her chest fall, but she wouldn't breathe on her own. His heart wrenched in pain as he tasted the coppery blood in her mouth and smelled the slight scent of burnt flesh.

"What have they done to my baby?" he cried out.

"Anthony, the medics are here. Let them attend to Ashley." Drake tried to move him away from his wife.

"No, I can't let her go."

"Come on, man. You got to let them help her." Roberto and Drake pulled Anthony up by his arms. He watched as the medics placed Ashley on the stretcher and quickly rolled her out to the waiting ambulance.

"I'm going with her," he said and moved to follow.

Drake and Roberto restrained him. "You can't," Drake said.

"The ambulance is taking her two blocks up the street to the chopper. Life flight couldn't land here so they're waiting for her up there. Come on and we'll meet them at the hospital. You can't ride in the chopper with her." Roberto escorted a bewildered Anthony out to their vehicle.

"I'll stay here and finish all the paperwork and keep the scene secured," Brease said as they reached the vehicle.

"Appreciate it," Drake replied.

"Keep me posted on Ashley," she called as they drove off.

Chapter 19

****

Jacksonville Medical Center
Friday Morning
12:45 a.m.

All during the ride to the hospital, Anthony had been silently praying for Ashley to be okay. Beside him, in the driver's seat, Drake sat elaborating on the success of the operation and how they had finally gotten Fox, only occasionally coming up for air.

His partner's nonstop flow of words bounced off Anthony's ears, hardly penetrating as he thought about the woman he loved, his wife
 dying because of this operation. And they still didn't have any news on Chase yet, either.

Ashley Cameron-Langston. It had been ten years ago when he'd first laid his eyes on her. Ten years and four months, but who's counting? He thought with a self-deprecating smile. She was the most beautiful, tantalizing, and bad-ass woman he had ever met. They'd had four good years before he left her to take out the Mafia leaders trying to kill her. He had hurt her badly, leaving with no explanation. After five years, fate had brought them back together and he had cherished every day of that time with her and their son.

Anthony squeezed his eyes shut, remembering how she smelled of salt-water and sea air every morning after they swam with A.J. His work had still taken him away too much. He had missed too much time with her and now he might never have that time again. He opened his eyes and glanced out the window, barely seeing the scenery go by as Drake took the streets much quicker than they were meant to be taken.

"What the hell? You haven't heard a word I said." Drake's voice finally elbowed its way through his thoughts, demanding his attention. Demanding a response.

Turning, Anthony looked at him. "What?"

"You," Drake repeated impatiently, turning a corner, and going down the drive that led them to the E.R.

entrance of the hospital. "I said, Ashley is a fighter. She will be fine."

Anthony stopped himself from bracing against the dashboard as Drake squealed to a stop at the ER entrance. "I pray you're right."

Drake snorted. "Don't give me that. You know she'll be okay. If she can handle the likes of you, she can make it through anything."

Drake had been his partner for years on and off, and he shared as much with him as he did any man. But right now he didn't feel like talking. He just wanted everything to magically be okay.

"Let's get inside to Ashley." Anthony was out of the car before he finished speaking.

"I'll be right in," Drake called after his retreating figure.

****

He found the registration desk and waited patiently for the clerk to hang up the phone. "Can you tell me where I can find Ashley Langston?" he asked.

"Sir, are you okay?" The receptionist asked, seeing Anthony's blood soaked shirt.

"I'm fine. Where is Ashley Langston?"

"Is she a patient, sir?"

"Yes, she just came in by life flight."

"Are you a family member?"

"Yes, I am her husband."

"Please have a seat in the waiting room down the hall. Someone will be out shortly to speak with you," she said, pointing down the hall.

Anthony walked around the corner and down the hallway to the emergency waiting area. He waited his body numb with fear. The relief he'd felt at finding her had been short-lived once he'd seen her condition. The team had moved as quickly as possible to secure her release and eliminate Fox. He just prayed they had gotten her help quick enough.

Ashley was alone. None of her family was with her, just medical staff. All those months ago, they had made the decision they would retire from criminal work, and look at them now. She was fighting for her life, and Chase was in critical condition.

Twenty minutes later, Drake joined him. "Any news?"

"No, they just told me to have a seat and someone would be with me shortly." He stared down at the stark white ceramic tiles.

"Roberto just got here. Grayson is going to the airport to wait for Brenda. Chase is undergoing his second surgery now. The doctors say he will be fine, just broken up pretty bad."

"Damn, everything just went to shit."

A young dark-haired man in a blue scrubs entered the waiting room. "Is there anyone here with the Langston family?" he asked.

Anthony stood up. "I'm her husband."

"I'm Dr. Kingston. Let's step down the hallway." Anthony followed Dr. Kingston into a small room just off the waiting area. "Your wife is in critical condition. She has some broken bones in her hands and feet where the electrical shocks caused violent muscle contractions. There are severe burns on the heels of her feet and the palms of her hands plus smaller ones that appear to be multiple contact points on her upper body, arms, and legs. EKG and CT scans revealed electrical shock to the brain occurred, which explains the seizures she is experiencing. Can you tell me how she received electrical shock injuries of this magnitude?" he asked.

"Undercover operation went bad. She was taken by the Mafia leader, tied to a chair, and shocked repeatedly for hours before we got to her."

"It just helps to know the nature of the injuries for me to provide the best care."

"Can I see her?" Anthony asked.

"We are still running some more tests; I'm concerned about her going into cardiac arrest. She is sedated right now to keep her calm and minimize the pain. I'm working with the worst burn areas first; some will require skin grafting. I will let you in to see her, so you can visit briefly."

"Thank you, doctor."

"Before you go in to visit with your wife, we will stop by my office and I will give you one of my scrub shirts to wear. The shirt you're wearing can't be worn in the unit."

Anthony looked down at his shirt, soaked in Fox's blood. "Thank you, again. Do everything you possibly can for her, please," he begged. He followed Dr. Kingston down to his office where he changed his shirt, bagging the one he had on for evidence.

"Right this way." Dr. Kingston said.

Anthony followed him through the double doors to the ER.

He thought his heart would break into when he saw Ashley. She looked so pale with her eyes closed, all bandaged up with a machine helping her breathe. Anthony bent over and gently kissed her on the cheek and lightly stroked the top of her hand. "I love you, baby. Everything will be okay. Ashley, don't leave me, don't leave me..."

All of a sudden, her body jerked and the machine to his right showed a flat line instead of the up and down of a regular heartbeat. "She's going into cardiac arrest. Clear the room. You must leave now and let us do our job," Dr. Kingston commanded as he began working on Ashley. An orderly quickly escorted Anthony out of the ER. He walked down the hallway and out the front doors. The weather had gotten bad.

"You, okay?" Drake asked.

"I just needed some air."

"I suppose you've noticed the rain is coming down in buckets? Or that you're wearing a scrub shirt?"

"The rain feels good, the doc wouldn't let me go in the ER to see Ashley with a blood soaked shirt." He shuddered.

"Of course, it feels wonderful," Drake said dryly, leaning against a concrete column, which supported the awning over the ER ambulance entrance. "There's nothing like getting drenched at 3 a.m. to purge the soul."

"I can't lose her, Drake. I can't lose her…" Anthony broke down.

"Man, she's gonna be okay."

"I'm sorry, I don't lose control… but she just went into cardiac arrest."

"It's okay. Something would be wrong with you if you didn't show emotion right now."

"She's in bad shape. Dr. Kingston made me leave the room." He punched the concrete column with his fist.

Drake grabbed him by the wrist of his injured hand to keep him from doing further damage. He turned Anthony to face him. "It's okay, man. It's going to be okay. You're not going to be any good to Ashley like this."

Anthony sobbed for a few seconds before quickly composing himself. "I'm okay."

Drake released his friend and patted him on the back again. "Let's go back in and see what we can find out, okay?"

"Okay," Anthony replied softly.

"We need to get one of the nurses to look at that hand of yours now, too."

"It's all right," Anthony replied as he looked at his busted, bleeding hand.

"Well, at least let them wrap it up so you don't drip damn blood everywhere. Besides, the doc isn't going to keep giving you clothes to wear."

Anthony fell silent for a few moments, his mind working feverishly. Ashley just had to pull through and be okay. "Fine, I'll see a nurse."

Chapter 20

****

It must have been near sunrise when the sound of seagulls woke Ashley. She opened her eyes to the brightest light she had ever seen. It felt so warm and inviting. She had been so cold but now she felt warm and safe. She drifted slowly toward the light. "Don't leave me... don't leave me." She heard Anthony's sweet voice so far away.

"Where am I?" She tried to focus on her surroundings.

She was floating further away toward a dark tunnel. Ashley closed her eyes and floated to the end. Once she came out, she saw beautiful flowers and trees. A crystal clear body of water glistened to my right. She reached down toward the water, feeling it run through her fingers. It felt cool as it flowed right through her fingers.

The fish were so brightly colored, their little bodies reflecting light as they swam above the pretty colored stones on the bottom. Ashley looked up into the huge tree, full of rich bronze colored leaves. Birds chirped and sang so sweetly. Two seagulls flew overhead; silver light shone from their wings.

There was a door at the other end, a short distance from the cool water. Through the large window at the top of the door, she could see vast green meadows and rolling hills. Golden light glistened off the hilltops. Ashley knew she should be going through that door, but wanted to enjoy the water just a moment longer. Something told her that, once she went through that arched doorway, there would be no returning. She felt so peaceful, content and more loved than I ever had in my whole life.

She heard a soft voice in her head say, "Ashley, you have to go back. It's not time yet."

Just a few more minutes.

Suddenly, everything went dark again.

"Mrs. Langston, Mrs. Langston, can you hear me? Nod your head if you can hear me. Mrs. Langston, can you hear me?"

Ashley slowly opened her eyes and gently nodded her head. She could hear the voice but everything was fuzzy. She felt disoriented and shivered, suddenly very cold. She looked down at the monitor hooked to her chest and IVs in both arms. Her hands and arms were bandaged and she could felt bandages on her feet under the sheet.

"You're going to be okay. You suffered a mild heart attack. Your husband is here waiting to see you."

Ashley nodded her head, unable to summon the energy to do anything else. She wanted to speak but couldn't, her eyes felt so heavy; she couldn't keep them open. Ashley tried hard to think, she couldn't remember how she'd ended up here in the hospital. Slowly, darkness took over again as she drifted into a deep sleep.

****

Anthony listened to the doctor talking as he stitched up the lacerations. He kept thinking he could have done more to protect Ashley. He should have known that Fox would go after her, should have known that Fox was behind the contract on her life…

"Okay, sir. You're good to go. Keep the area dry and see your doctor to remove the stitches in ten days." The doctor snapped his gloves off and shook his hand.

"Thanks, doc."

There was a tap on the door. Anthony leaped to his feet and yanked it open. "Oh, Drake. It's you. Is Ashley okay?"

"Yeah, it's me. You didn't think I would just leave you here, did you? Dr. Kingston just came through. He says you can go in and see Ashley for a short time only. But he wants to talk to you first."

"Okay, let's go. Where is he?" Anthony asked.

"He said for you to come to the nurses' station and they would page him," Drake replied.

They headed to the nurses' station and requested that Dr. Kingston be paged. Anthony stared down at the stark white tiles in the waiting
room. It seemed like an eternity before Dr. Kingston arrived.

"Mr. Langston, Mr. Drake." He shook both their hands and motioned for them to sit back down as he took a seat next to them. "Your wife is in stable condition but we have her heavily sedated. She suffered a mild heart attack due to the electrical shocks she endured."

"Is she going to be okay?" Anthony asked.

"In time, she should make a full recovery. She's in a lot of pain due to the extensive burns to her extremities as well as the broken bones. I need your permission to perform surgery to set the bones in her hands and feet. I will do the skin grafts to those areas at the same time." He glanced down at his watch. "I would like to begin the surgery at within the next few hours."

"Is it safe to do surgery now? If she just suffered a heart attack..." Anthony asked.

"We don't have a choice. If we don't treat the burn areas quickly, there is a risk of infection setting in."

"Can I see her now?"

"Yes, I will take you to her." Dr. Kingston stood.

Anthony looked back at Drake. "Are you coming?"

"No, I'll wait here. I'm going to find Roberto and see how Chase is doing. Grayson should be here with Brenda shortly."

Anthony followed the doctor down the hallway and into the Critical Care Unit. Ashley was in the bed, with a white sheet over her long slender body. Her pale, bandaged arms lay on top of the cover. IVs were still hooked to both arms. The tubes had been removed from her throat and she seemed to be breathing easier.

Anthony slowly walked closer to the edge of the bed. "Ashley, I'm here. I love you, baby.

Everything is going to be okay. You're going to be better soon and I'm taking you home to A.J." He squeezed his eyes tightly closed as a single tear found its way down his cheek.

"Do I have your permission to perform the surgery?" Dr. Kingston asked.

"Yes," Anthony answered in a quivering voice. "Doc, she is my whole world."

"I know. I will do everything I can. The surgery will take at least three to four hours. I'll have my assistant keep you posted on the progress throughout the procedure. She is a very strong and determined young lady. I feel that she will come through fine."

"Baby, I'm sorry I didn't protect you better," Anthony said. "I know you can hear me. I love you. We've got the best of our life ahead of us. I'll never leave your side again."

Thirty minutes later, Anthony still sat by Ashley's bed ever so gently holding her hand.

"Mr. Langston. We need to prep your wife for surgery now," a nurse informed him.

"Okay. I'll be in the waiting room." Anthony slowly stood up, kissed Ashley on the cheek before walking toward the door. He looked back one last time and walked out of the unit and down the hallway. He made a quick phone call to check on A.J., who was still asleep. He promised Morgan he would keep them posted. A few minutes later, he entered the waiting room to find Roberto talking to Drake.

"How are you holding up?" Roberto asked.

"Hanging in there. Ashley goes into surgery in about an hour. How's Chase?"

"Out of his second surgery and in recovery now. Grayson just got here with Brenda and Craig. Oh yeah, I had Grayson pick this up from our plane when they landed." Drake tossed a duffle bag at Anthony's feet.

"What's this?"

"Well, it's your bag… so I assume it is your clothes. I asked the nurses station if there was somewhere you could clean up. I figured you would be here awhile." Drake said.

"Thanks, man. I appreciate it."

"Anytime."

"Any word on how Director Jones is doing?" Anthony asked.

"Madison called earlier and said Jones is going to be fine."

"That's good. We've lost too many men already." Anthony shook his head.

Drake turned to Anthony. "We also have the last piece of the puzzle. Madison was able to talk to Jones. The leak at the governor's office was an agent in training who worked there about eight months ago. The agent breached the files containing all of Ashley's information and gave the information to Fox. Apparently, the intern's father had an astronomical gambling debt with Fox. Fox offered to wash the debt in exchange for any information on Ashley."

"I hope they have that fucking bastard in custody," Anthony said through gritted teeth.

"No. He's dead, along with his father."

"What?"

"An automobile accident. The brakes failed and they went over an embankment into the ocean." Drake shook his head.

"What the hell?"

"Probably not an accident, since it happened the day before the chopper ambushed the team. Fox would've eliminated anyone who could implicate him or provide information that would stop his plans to kill Ashley."

"How did Jones find out?" Anthony asked.

"He pulled together a team to go through all personnel files of everyone employed in any capacity over the past two years. Jones then leaked the information the day before you guys met."

"Holy shit." Anthony paced back and forth in the waiting room.

"My team just confirmed that the Black Hawk was stolen by the Cartel. That explains the hit on Jones, with Fox's Dixie Mafia and the Martinelli Colombian Drug Cartel linked by blood."

"Fox was one more evil bastard," Anthony muttered.

Drake slapped Anthony on the back. "He can't hurt anyone ever again. You sliced him open."

"Ashley wouldn't have stood a chance if you weren't an expert marksman. You took out the controller in the room behind her, quicker than I could blink."

"She's a fighter. She'll be okay. I'll hang out here with you a little while."

"Thanks, man." He continued to pace back and forth.

"I'm going to go check on Chase. He's up on the next floor," Roberto said.

"Okay. Keep us posted."

"You do the same."

Drake got a call and walked away.

"Will do. Talk to you soon," Drake replied before ending the call.

Drake walked back over to Anthony. "That was Brease. She called to check on Ashley and Chase. She's pulled an all-nighter and is still at the scene finishing up paperwork." "She's a good kid. She just doesn't have the stomach for fieldwork."

"She did say she had kept Director Madison updated and he wanted to know if you wanted him to fly out here."

"No need for him to come. As soon as Ashley is stable, I'm taking her home. I prefer doctors we know."

A male in scrubs entered the waiting room and approached. "Dr. Kingston asked me to let you know that the surgery on your wife is progressing well."

"Thank you," Anthony said.

"You're welcome. I will return shortly with another update."

"All we can do now is wait, and pray," Anthony said, leaning over and placing his head in his hands.

Chapter 21

The following three weeks were like scenes in one of the classic black-and-white movies Ashley loved to rent and cry over on the weekends. Anthony was attentive to her every need. The skin grafts were successful and her burns and broken bones were healing nicely. He had brought in a laptop equipped with a webcam so she could see and talk to A.J.

Finally, she was being discharged could go home. Home sounded wonderful.

She glanced over at the huge bouquet of fresh yellow roses on the stand beside her bed and smiled to herself. He was back to yellow. When she'd first came out of surgery and woken up in

her room, there was a huge bouquet of yellow roses. Every four to five days, they had changed; pink, white, red, and now yellow again.

"Hey, sunshine. You awake?" Anthony asked, getting up from the recliner beside her bed.

"Yep. I couldn't sleep for your loud snoring," she teased.

"Oh. I'm sorry, honey."

"I was kidding. Who stole your sense of humor?"

"Honestly? The job! I thought I had lost you this time. We can't go through this again."

"I know. I want to ask you something, Anthony," she said softly.

"Sure, honey."

"Can we go back to our house in Florida for a while? It's really home, and is very special to me because our bosses gave it to us as a wedding gift. We really haven't been able to enjoy being there for long..."

"I'm a step ahead of you, honey. I've already talked to Dr. Kingston about setting up your physical therapy and follow-up appointments
with our doctors in Bay of Sands." Anthony smiled.

"You're awesome."

"I have another surprise for you. Drake is flying A.J., your aunt, and uncle to Bay of Sands this afternoon. They'll be there waiting for us when we get home."

She glanced up at him with tears in her eyes. "I love you."

"I love you, too."

"What about Leo?" she asked.

Anthony laughed. "Yes, dear. Your crazy German Shepherd is flying home with A. J."

She smiled. There was a tap on the door. "Come in," Anthony said, sitting back down in the recliner.

"Hey, guys. We dropped in to say bye." Brenda pushed Chase's wheelchair up to the edge of Ashley's bed. Craig followed closely behind his parents.

"You look like crap, man," Ashley teased Chase.

"Well, you're not looking so great yourself."

"How long will you be in the cast?"

"Another two weeks. I'll be stuck in this damn wheelchair," he grunted.

"I'll finally have you totally captive." Brenda laughed, rubbing him on the arm.

"Honey, you don't need me in a wheelchair to have me captive." He kissed his wife on the hand.

"Geez." Craig snorted before walking over to sit on the side of Ashley's bed.

"Well, you guys can come visit us. After all, the house in Bay of Sands has a wheelchair ramp in the back."

"Oh, Ash. You and Anthony are going home to Florida?" Brenda asked.

"Yes, Anthony has taken care of everything."

"I'm so glad. We can all hang out like old times."

"Did Drake take care of getting you home?" Anthony asked Chase.

"He's arranged everything. One of his private jets is waiting at the airport to fly us home now. Roberto is going to pick us up at the airport."

They visited for another hour before saying their goodbyes. "Aunt Ash, I love you." Craig kissed Ashley on the cheek before quickly following his mom and dad out of the room.

"I'm sure all of this has been really hard on Craig. He's still a teenager, yet old enough to understand everything. A senior in high school and he has to grow up so fast." Ashley frowned.

"You look worn out, babe. Try to get some rest. We've got a long afternoon once you get released. We have to drive to the airport, fly to Bay of Sands, and then drive home."

"Okay, I do feel tired," she said as her eyes slowly closed and she drifted off to sleep.

****

The sigh that escaped her lips seemed to come from deep down in her soul. She still hadn't gained all her strength back. Anthony glanced at her before looking back to the road. "Tired?"

There was a time when she'd thought the trip was never going to end. She ached all over but was surprised that her head wasn't throbbing as it had for weeks. The smile she offered him was weary. "I feel as if someone has dissected me, then put me back together with a very blunt needle and fishing line."

The light turned red. He gave her a deep stare. "Well, they did an amazing job. You look fantastic."

Instinctively she touched his cheek, love filtering through her. "Thanks, I needed that."

The light turned green and he eased his foot back on the accelerator. "Anything you need. I'm here for you."

"I know." She let his words comfort her.

"The freeway connection is just ahead. Do you need to stop for anything before we get on it?"

She just wanted to go somewhere she felt safe. "No, straight home is fine." She stared at his profile. "I just need to hold our son."

He understood what she meant. "He's an awesome kid." His own words echoed back to him and he grinned. "I never thought I'd hear myself say that about someone who doesn't even come up to my belt buckle, but he really is." He pulled onto the freeway ramp.

"You did a great job raising him without me those first years."

"Don't sing the praises too soon, we still have a work in progress," she reminded him. "He isn't a teenager yet."

"I gave my father some hell before I settled down. A.J. is going to be the best."

Ashley settled back in the seat and closed her eyes. Less than an hour later, Anthony brought the car to a stop in the driveway of their home. He glanced over at the sleeping figure of his wife.

"Honey, we're home," he said gently, touching her on the arm.

"Okay." She tried to rouse herself. "I guess I dozed off."

"Dozed off? You were snoring like a freight train." He laughed.

"I guess I learned that trick from you." She smiled, flashing perfectly white teeth.

"Wait there and I'll come around and get you out of the car."

She opened the passenger door. "I can get myself out of the car."

"I know you can, dear. But, you're not going to," Anthony said softly. He effortlessly reached down and picked her up out of the passenger seat, walking with ease up the steps to the front door of their home. The front door opened when he was three feet away.

"Oh, my sweet girl." Morgan opened the door wide.

Anthony laid Ashley down gently on the sofa. "Sweetheart, are you okay?" Aunt Lynn asked.

"Yes, I'm fine. Just a little tired from the trip. Where's A. J.?"

"He just fell asleep. He tried so hard to stay awake."

"We've been so worried about you," Morgan said.

They all turned to the sound of whining and scratching coming from the other side of the kitchen door. Anthony walked over and opened the door. "Easy, boy."

Leo made a beeline for the sofa, whining, barking, and licking Ashley softly all over her face. It was almost like Leo knew she wasn't completely well.

"I missed you, too," she said, patting Leo on the head as he continued to whine.

"Momma, Momma, Momma," A. J. squealed, running down the stairs.

"Oh, A .J. I missed you so much." She threw her arms around him and squeezed him tight.

"Me and Leo went to bed. I told Leo to let me know when you got home."

"You did?" Ashley ruffled her son's hair.

"Yep and when I heard him barking, I knew you were home." A.J. smiled.

"Well, Leo did what you asked."

"Daddy, Daddy." A. J. ran from the sofa to Anthony. He lifted A.J. up and twirled him in the air. "I missed you, buddy."

"I missed you, too." A. J. threw his arms around Anthony's neck.

"Is anyone hungry? I can warm up dinner?" Lynn asked.

"I just want to crawl in my bed and go to sleep." Ashley smiled weakly.

"How about I take you upstairs and get you all settled? A.J. and I will serve you dinner in bed in a little while," Anthony suggested.

"Okay. This is one time I'm not going to argue."

"Honey, the day you stop arguing with me... I will really worry." Tony said as he scooped her up and headed up the stairs.

****

Hours later, all snuggled up in bed, Anthony glanced down at his beautiful sleeping wife. On his other side, clinging to his arm was his sweet son. He kissed them each gently on the cheek. His feet were numb from the weight of Leo, crashed out on the foot of the bed. We have to invest in a king-sized bed, Anthony thought as he eased his arm away from A.J., reached over, and turned off the light.

Epilogue

Ten Months Later
Bay of Sands, Florida
6:00 a.m.

Ashley awakened early and slid quietly out of bed, careful not to wake Anthony. She walked softly down the hallway and peeked in on A.J., who was still fast asleep. Leo lifted his head and jumped off the bed, wagging his tail at the sight of her. Downstairs, she opened the refrigerator and pulled out a container of freshly squeezed orange juice, filled a glass, and walked out onto the deck to enjoy the view.

The sun was up and the promise of an early summer scorcher was evident in the air. The gentle salty breeze from the ocean smelled like Heaven. She let the last of the cold liquid slide down her throat and decided it was a nice morning for a walk on the beach.

She stepped inside, retrieving her cell phone from the counter. She slid it in her back pocket and tucked the .32 in her waistband. Easing out the front door, she made her way down to the beach with Leo close on her heals.

It felt so good to walk in the sand and feel the cool granules beneath her feet. Her injuries had healed nicely after two more surgeries and three months of physical therapy. The bottom of her feet were still a little tender, so the cool gulf water felt great caressing her skin. Her nightmares were seldom now. The Mafia and Cartel were no longer
a threat to her family. Anthony had been offered a promotion with the CIA and had rejected the position. He, instead, had taken the position of director of the law enforcement academy. It was only an hour away, so he was home every night. Ashley still ran her private investigations business, but she'd hired several investigators and did very little field work. She worked from home and spent time with A. J. and Leo.

The salty ocean air brought renewed strength to her body. Ashley jogged up the beach feeling the cool ocean breeze caressing her skin. The sky was painted in a million magnificent colors of orange as the sun blessed another day.

She and Leo stopped jogging and had walked only a short distance back down the beach when her cell phone began ringing. She slipped the phone out of her pocket, thinking it was Anthony. "Yes, dear."

"Morning, Ash. I know it's early, but I couldn't wait a second longer to call you," Gina Rae said.

"Are you okay? You sound out of breath."

"I'm better than okay. You'll never, never guess?" Gina Rae giggled into the phone.

"What, tell me?" Ashley said.

"I'm pregnant, I'm pregnant." Gina Rae said with excitement.

"Oh, I'm so happy for you and Larry."

"I'm eight weeks along. We wanted to make sure everything was okay before telling anyone. I told Larry I had to call you."

"I can't wait to tell Anthony, What did Larry say?" Ashley said.

"I thought I was going to have to call the damn

paramedics to start with… he just stood there staring at me for a few seconds. He is so happy and can't wait to be a daddy."

"It is a bit of shock, even when it is planned." Ashley laughed.

"How are you doing?" Gina Rae asked.

"Good. A.J. is getting bigger every day. Chase and Brenda came over for dinner last night. Chase has fully recovered. Their son, Craig, started college."

"How are your aunt and uncle?"

"They're doing great. We're going down to visit when Anthony is off work for summer break."

"I can't wait to see you guys. I'll call you later. Love you, girl," Gina Rae said.

"I love you, too. Congratulations and Bye." Ashley ended the call and slid her phone back in her pocket, hiding a secret smile.

She turned to walk back up the beach toward their home, throwing a Frisbee for Leo.

In the distance, she saw Anthony jogging down the beach toward her.

He still looked awesome. Ashley admired his strong broad shoulders, golden body, and dark hair.

When he reached her, he had a panicked look in his eyes. "Are you okay?" he asked.

"Yes, I just came out for a walk and didn't want to wake you guys." Her lashes swept up.

Her left hand lifted and pressed lightly against the line of his jaw. "Anthony, I love you, but you worry too much."

"I don't like waking up and not having you in bed beside me." He kissed her. He needed her too much. Always had. The pain of the past didn't matter; she was with him now. In his arms. It still terrified him when he woke up and she wasn't next to him. He wanted to spend the rest of his life making her happy, keeping her safe, hearing her laugh, and seeing the sparkle in her blue eyes. He wanted forever with her and A.J.

She kissed him deeply and her head dipped toward him. "You do make me so happy." She stared up at him, her heart shining in her eyes.

His grin matched hers. "Have I told you lately that I love you?"

"I don't think so. Not in the last three minutes." Ashley laughed. He slid his arm around her waist as they walked back up the beach. "Oh, I have great news," she said.

"What?"

"Gina Rae called and she's pregnant."

"A little Larry running around? Oh my lord." Anthony laughed.

"I have even better news."

They stopped at the foot of the walkway heading up to their back deck. Anthony stared down at his wife's glowing face. "What's up?"

"Well, we haven't really talked about this, so I don't know how you're going to feel. I was quite surprised myself…" She hesitated, nervous.

"Honey, what wrong?" he asked.

"Nothing is wrong. It's just that… I'm pregnant, too."

Anthony was speechless for a few seconds before wrapping his arms around Ashley and lifting her up and spinning her around in the air. Leo ran in circles around them, barking and kicking sand up everywhere.

"Okay, Leo, okay. I'm putting your momma down." Anthony laughed.

"Are you happy about the baby?" Ashley asked.

Anthony's gaze settled on his wife. With his heart overflowing with joy, he reached for her hand, bringing it gently to his lips. "I couldn't be happier. I love you. We've been so blessed."

"Twice blessed. I love you, too," she said as they walked hand in hand up the stairs to tell A.J. the good news.

"You know A.J. has wanted a little sister," Anthony said.

"Oh, really?"

"Yep, he's mentioned it to me several times."

"Well, if he doesn't get his wish this time... We can always try again." Ashley glanced up at her husband again, amusement shining in her eyes.

Anthony smiled, flashing perfectly white teeth. "And, oh, the fun we will have trying."

It had been a long time coming, but Ashley and Anthony Langston had weathered the crossroads to Hell and arrived in Heaven. Justice wasn't the only thing that was eternal...

So was their love.

ABOUT THE AUTHOR

R. L. Dodson grew up in southern Alabama and holds a B.S. in History and Criminal Justice. She has spent almost twenty years working in the Criminal Justice Arena. From an early age, she loved to read and later wrote poetry and short stories. She hopes that you enjoy taking this journey through the "Justice" series books.

R. L. resides in Florida.

"Eternal Justice" is the sequel to
"Heart of Jaded Justice"

She loves to hear from her readers.

Visit her at:
rl.dodson@yahoo.com

https:www.facebook.com/RLDodsonAuthor

https://twitter.com/RLDodson1